WE AREN'T FINISHED SURVIVING

GABRIELLA GANEM

Editor: Taylor Hale (www.hale-editorial.com)
Beta Reader: Belle Z. Orchade (www.fiverr.com/bellezorchade)
Book Formatting: Books and Moods (www.booksandmoods.com)
Cover Photo: Malachai Brooks (Unsplash)
Author Photographer: Carsten Tice (www.carstentice.com)

ISBN: 978-0-578-39825-9

A note from the author about the content of this book:

Please note that this book discusses and may depict topics such as **PTSD, anxiety, depression, abandonment, domestic and physical abuse, parent death, car accidents, trauma, scars, nightmares about traumatic events, injury, and panic attacks.**

I, the author, have done my best to approach these topics with sensitivity, but if you feel this kind of content may be triggering to you, the reader, **please be aware and consider putting this book down.**

If you choose to continue and at any point you feel affected or distressed, please put the book down, take a deep breath, and do something that makes you happy.

If at any point you feel the need to talk to someone about these issues, please phone a friend, a parent, a sibling, a teacher, or someone you trust.

For those who have been hurt and
choose to keep surviving.
For the hopeless romantics, myself included.
And for Kerby. You always told me I'd write a
book; I guess you were right :)

THE PLAYLIST:

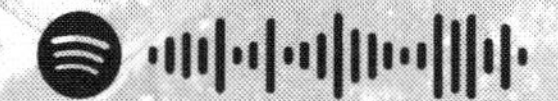

"Come a Little Closer" by Cage the Elephant
"Fine Line" by Harry Styles
"Wait" by M83
"No Light, No Light" by Florence + The Machine
"Hold On" by Chord Overstreet
"Overjoyed" by Matchbox Twenty
"exile" by Taylor Swift (feat. Bon Iver)
"Fire Meet Gasoline" by Sia
"when i'm with you" by We Three
"Dive" by Luke Combs
"Turning Page (Instrumental)" by Sleeping At Last
"Bucket List" by Mitchell Tenpenny
"Gravity" by Sara Bareilles
"I Go Away" by MNDR
"Take on the World" by You Me At Six
"Fall" by Ed Sheeran
"You Found Me" by The Fray
"Secrets" by OneRepublic
"Love I'm Given" by Ellie Goulding
"Perfect Harmony" by Madison Reyes and Charlie Gillespie
"arms" by Christina Perri
"Kiss Me Slowly" by Parachute
"Unconditionally" by Katy Perry
"I Do" by Aloe Blac
"Home Sweet" by Russell Dickerson

Chapter 1

The snow has always been a reminder of home to me. From a very early age, I would eagerly await the day winter officially began so I could see the first snowfall of the year. When I turned five, I was finally old enough to snowboard, and I couldn't get enough of it. As the years passed and I moved into middle-school, I started to snowboard competitively, which both terrified my parents and made them proud of me. They didn't want their only son to end up injured—or worse—on the slopes, but they continued to support me because they knew how much snowboarding meant to me.

After my first breakup, I went outside and lied in the snow—and when my grandfather died, I did the same. The wind whipped around my body, making a howling noise that drowned my inner thoughts and helped me escape the world for just a moment. The cold would sting my ears and cheeks, and yet the pain allowed me to feel reality exactly how I needed to.

Year after year, my heart yearned for the fall leaves to fade and the first flurries of the season to fly in. My home. My refuge.

After the accident, I couldn't remember where my home was. What I had once loved so dearly had been tainted by my fear and my anxiety. I changed. The snow changed its meaning for me. *Maybe forever.*

Chapter 2
Before

"I thought driving down the *Million Dollar Highway,* I would at least see some famous celebrities." Lydia's voice feigns annoyance, and I hear Andrew snicker in the front of the car.

I roll my eyes, turning to face the girl sitting opposite of me in the back of my brother's car. "Lydia, the name of the highway refers to the amount of money it took to build it, not that every time you drive along it you'll see Robert Pattinson or Harry Styles."

She narrows her eyes and shakes her head jokingly but turns back around to look out at the road. When Andrew made several wrong turns on our drive from Utah State University, what was supposed to be a six-hour drive became a spontaneous drive through Durango, Colorado, and now onto the Million Dollar Highway. My twin brother might share the same genes and looks as me—both of us being hazel eyed with dark brown hair and six-feet tall—but he does not share my sense of direction. While none of us particularly want to be driving on this road at this time of the year—it's too dangerous with the narrow, icy roads and low visibility—our rental house is too close to turn around now.

Lydia has been making little comments here and there about random news, thoughts that pop into her head and who knows what else. When we decided to drive up to Montrose for a week before heading home to our parents' house for winter break, I knew Lydia would keep us occupied. Andrew invited his best friend Lucas to join us, and he sits next to him in the front of the car on his phone. Lydia tagged along since her parents were out of the country, and we also invited Brooke. I was surprised Brooke chose to come along since I had assumed she had other plans for winter break. She volunteered to sit in the middle, next to me in the back, since she is the smallest out of the five of us.

Brooke is quite beautiful, not just pretty. She has the features, of course—piercing blue eyes, long chestnut hair—but her personality is what's magnetic about her. If she were interested, I know half of the guys in the school would still be lining up to take her out. I'm not sure why she isn't.

Seeing her backpack on the floor of the car slightly open, revealing a tattered copy of *Wuthering Heights*, I am reminded of when I first noticed her love for reading. It was in our first class together. I had been placed in an upper-division English course our first year of college because I had enough credits for the lower-level courses. I was surprised to see, however, that

I wasn't the only freshman in that class, and that Brooke was also in it.

My surprise was overturned quickly when I heard how she spoke in class. We were reading some difficult course materials, even for those at par in the class, but Brooke spoke about them as though she knew the author, their intent, their purpose.

Then after class, she'd be sitting under one of the trees by the lecture hall, not reading our course material—rather, it was always something different. Philosophy, science textbooks, mysteries. Every time I passed her, I always wondered if she was going to be an English major. She sure seemed to be interested enough.

I gathered that she is more closed off when five of the guys on the snowboarding team tried to ask her out and she told them she wasn't interested in dating someone she hardly knew and just wanted to be with her friends. Each guy returned, talking about how she obviously had to have been lying, since their egos were hurt, but she didn't seem like the type to me. After Jaden, the captain of the snowboarding team, tried last, no one else attempted.

Lydia came into the picture around the end of our first semester. The platinum-haired girl with brown eyes was transferring in from some school in Arizona, but she had lived in Utah her whole life, so she knew a lot of the people at our school. Quickly, she rose to high popularity, and not in an arrogant way. Even now, she is still one of those people you wonder how they can be so nice.

The next semester, I needed to take biology, and both Brooke and Lydia were in that class. Andrew sat next to me for most of it, bored out of his mind, which made sense since he was only taking this class as a fulfillment for his science requirement. Andrew is a film major, so while he loves movies that have science aspects to them, he could care less about mitosis. Still, my twin has got to be one of the most determined people when it comes to school, seeing as he passed the class with a higher grade than I did.

I didn't mind the class as much as my brother, mostly because I like processes and there are quite a few of those in biology. I gained an appreciation for those going into the field because of the rigor, but I was especially glad I am a psychology major after finishing the class.

While my brother and I had a little more of a difficult time with the class, Brooke stayed focused and attentive as usual, and I got to realize that Lydia did the same. They became fast friends, Lydia joining Brooke under her favorite tree. Everyone left the tree open from three until five so that Brooke and Lydia could enjoy it. I guess that comes with being genuinely nice; people want to do good things for you.

After the second semester, we all went home for summer, and when we came back this fall, I saw Brooke a little bit more. Lydia and Lucas started dating over the summer after they had gotten to know each other in one of their classes. They had been paired together because there hadn't been any other elementary education majors or business administration majors in the class, and all the time they spent together in class started to spill to outside of class.

The two being together only meant that Brooke was around more often. Lydia didn't force her on us, and she also didn't force us on her. Brooke started to get more comfortable with us over the past few months, and now, we're all under that tree from three until five. Sometimes I'll even play my guitar when I'm bored, and people will request songs.

When I started to sit at the tree with her more often, I saw why my teammates felt they needed to save-face after Brooke rejected them—she is incredibly beautiful, wickedly smart, and kind. I found myself eager to get to the tree, to hear Brooke talk about any part of her day, and when she was sick and couldn't make it to meet with us, I found myself feeling disappointed. I barely knew her major, and I was already captivated by her.

Andrew started to notice since I was, according to him, "painfully obvious about my feelings". When I talked about how I felt, he said, "Jackson, you're screwed." I am fully aware, and I tried to avoid her just a little so that my infatuation could subside a little bit. It was, however, impossible to stay away, so I gave up, justifying my decision by saying that we are in the same friend-group. I was more worried that she would think I hated her because I wasn't around as much, which was the furthest thing from the truth.

Even now, with her next to me I still worry that her silence is because she thinks I am trying to avoid her. I feel bad, not sure if she's excited to be spending five days in the mountains with us based on her silence, but self-consciously I wonder if she feels apprehensive around me. Even if she doesn't feel bothered by my avoidance, she probably caught onto my "painfully obvious" feelings for her, and that might have made her feel weird.

I close my eyes and try to listen to the hum of the tires on the road, but the highway is too winding for me to relax. I go to grab some water to settle my stomach, but when I reach for a bottle from the twenty-four pack Lucas insisted on purchasing before we left, another hand meets mine. I look to my left and see Brooke also looking at me. She quickly grabs a water and sits back in her seat.

Internally, I frown. I can't help but feel as though she's avoiding me now, and I kick myself for making her feel awkward. When I sit back in my seat, I keep my eyes on her, hoping that she'll maybe speak to me, and I can promise her that I in no way have feelings for her and am content with being her friend. *Lies.* I guess she must have felt my eyes on her because she takes out her phone, taps something, and then turns to me with a questioning innocence and says, "Yes?"

"Brooke," I start, unsure of how to approach her clear avoidance of me. "I feel like I might have done something to make you feel awkward around me. If I did, can you tell me what I did so I can assure you that I didn't mean to?" *Like purposefully avoid you for a few days so I could stop thinking about you for two seconds.* I expect to hear her say that I did make her feel weird and prepare to have Andrew glance at me in the rearview mirror with a smirk on his face. However, there is a glint of humor in her eyes.

She turns to Lydia and says, "I told you he was going to think he did something wrong." Confusion must be visible on my face when she turns back because she answers, "I have AirPods in and have been listening to music." She pulls back her hair to reveal the white headphones, small enough to be hidden behind her hair. "When Lydia and I were driving to you and your brother's apartment, I was telling her I wanted to listen to music because it distracts me from getting carsick, but I didn't want you guys to think something was wrong or that I didn't like you guys." She playfully hits Lydia's shoulder. "Lydia said it would be fine, so I've been listening to music."

Internally, I sigh now understanding why she has been so silent the entire ride. "So, I didn't do anything?" I clarify. *She isn't avoiding me?*

She lips turn upwards. "No, Jackson. You didn't do anything."

That smile. "Well, I don't want you to get carsick, so you can listen to your music instead of me."

She grins at me, but before she starts the music again, she leans forward to ask my twin a question. "Andrew, do you happen to know how much longer we have until we get to Montrose?"

He shrugs. "I'd say we only have an hour and a half left if the snow doesn't cause any worse traffic." Snow coats the road and rains down from the afternoon sky, and we didn't anticipate coming this way, so I wouldn't be surprised if it took longer than that.

Brooke leans back into her seat and opens her phone to select some music. I notice she has quite a few playlists with some odd names, some with really long names, and some that make normal playlist names sound like the title of a Panic! at the Disco or Fallout Boy song. She must have noticed I was looking at her music, because she gives me a look that instantly makes me feel guilty. But then she starts laughing.

"You should've seen your face—you looked like you killed

my dog and I found out!" When she stops laughing so hard, she turns her phone to me. "I know my playlists are a little eclectically titled, but I like them being a bit different. Plus, they actually do make sense in certain circumstances." She scrolls down to one titled *driving with the top down.*

"I like this one for when I need to have a little more energy. These songs never fail to get my energy up, and none of them are skip songs."

My eyebrows furrow. "Skip songs?"

"Yeah, skip songs are songs that you can listen to, but sometimes when they play, you just don't want to listen to them." She scrolls down to one titled, *I'm not from the south but I like to say y'all.* This one makes me laugh.

She grins, a little wider than normal, before saying, "Hey, anyone who knows me knows that I like country a lot, and I obviously wouldn't be a true music lover if I didn't have a playlist for my country songs." When I see the songs on this playlist with artists ranging from well-known country artists to lesser known, plus some artists I don't even recognize, I see she is serious.

"I'm assuming none of these are skip songs either," I say, still slightly laughing.

"You would be correct. Honestly, none of my playlists have skips. But not all of them have really long titles," she says, looking for a specific playlist now. I see her open one called *crashbash,* and unlike the other two, I am not exactly sure what it means.

She goes on, "I like listening to music or rain noises to help me fall asleep. This is a playlist with music that I can listen to that isn't too loud. It's a crash, like I'm going to go crash, and bash because it still has music."

My lips quirk upwards slightly at her childish obsession with these playlists. It's adorable. I also notice one above this playlist titled *existential at 3 am.* Curious, I ask, "What is that one for?"

She doesn't immediately respond, which only makes me more curious. "Well, don't take this the wrong way, but I use that one to cry." I can tell she is a little embarrassed, but I silently urge her to continue. "I don't always sleep that well and sometimes it helps to get some emotions out to relax more. This one helps me to feel those emotions." She looks away for a second, but then back at me, her eyes saying something that isn't quite readable.

I don't push her because I can see that while she was just honest with me, there is more behind that story, and I don't want to make her feel any more awkward. She isn't ready to share it, and that's okay, even though I want to know everything about her.

"So," I say, trying to change the subject slightly. "Do you make playlists for people?"

Her earlier smile turns to a genuine one, and I feel a grin tugging at my own lips.

"I do, sometimes, but usually only for people that mean the most to me. I have to know who they are and what kind of music would speak to them before I make one, you know what I mean?" She cocks her head slightly.

"Yeah," I breathe. *I want to be one of those people.*

She squints slightly and opens her mouth to say something,

but all of the sudden Lydia screams. Andrew starts yelling and Lucas's phone is thrown on the roof with a bang. I look at Lydia and try to see why she is screaming, following her eyesight. Then, I see it.

It's like time has stood still. My first thought is this is how it ends, staring down the grill of an SUV. At the moment, I feel like I have forever to wait for impact, but just as soon as I think this, the front of the SUV collides with us and we're flipped on our side.

Once. Twice. And then the ground is visible out of the front windshield. The ground you pray never to see when driving on a mountain, the bottom of a cliff. A drop at least one-hundred feet below. I hope to see something—anything—that would come close to resembling safety. But nothing is here. Nothing is going to be here.

And then we're going over the mountainside. It is the truest of nightmares, the fear I always had when driving up or down a mountain as a kid. We weren't supposed to even be here. Now, we're going to die.

I look at my brother and hope that he hears me try to yell, "I love you," to him, even though my throat cannot force the noise out. I never said it enough. I never said it enough to my sisters, to my mother. Would it be easier here and now if I had? Would there ever be enough *I love yous* for them to survive me? To survive Andrew?

The car jerks and reals me back to reality. We toss and turn in our seats, and I am jammed against the ceiling hard. Lydia is the only one who screams loud enough for me to hear her as her arm slams against the seat. Lucas is trying to yell and break free. We all know what is happening.

Brooke looks at me with wide eyes and grabs my hand, clasping mine to hers as though that alone will save us. I pull her to me, hugging her to hopefully protect her from the impending impact we are expecting.

In that moment, all that I know is that I am here, with Brooke in my arms, praying to not die. *I don't want to die. I don't want her to die.* I barely hear the screams around me over the wind blowing through the cracked windows. I know it won't do me any good to add to them. What's the point?

I'm so close to Brooke that my nose is buried in her hair, and I realize it smells like flowers. What a weird thing to note about this girl at a time like this. But the thing is that right now, I feel like I have known her forever.

"It's okay, Brooke," I try to whisper into her hair. I'm lying, of course, but if my lie can soothe her at all, I'll feel like I won. The car jams against the side of the mountain again, and she whimpers in my arms.

I think Lydia has stopped screaming. That scares me. That means she has given up or passed out. I look over to her passed out next to Brooke, and then look at Andrew in the rearview mirror, time still feeling like it is at a standstill, and he looks at me. He smiles. I force one back. Both are painful.

I look out the window, seeing the snowy mountains and the trees that pass us by fast. It's a beautiful place to die. No one else was on the road other than the car that hit us, so no one saw us. Everyone else was smart enough to avoid this road this time of year. We didn't.

I look at the snow, reminded of my love for it. The beauty

of my board gliding along and how my body moved like it was made for it. I loved it. I still love it. I fear it.

I take one last look at my brother, and one more look at the girl in my arms. She mouths the words, *"Thank you."* I know confusion passes over my face, although I assume she means for trying to protect her. What else could it mean? We're all about to die.

My arms wrap tighter around her, around her neck in hopes of stunting her pain. A weird peace floats over me as I close my eyes.

This is the end.

Even with my eyes closed, I know that the ground is getting closer and closer. There are trees being crushed below us and rocks bumping against the side of our car.

My head is slammed against the ceiling once more, but I don't let go of Brooke. *I'll never let go.*

And then I slip into the darkness.

Chapter 3
After

TWO WEEKS AFTER THE CRASH

Today is the day I get to go home.

I have been at Johnson Memorial Hospital for eight days now, and I have been counting down the hours until I can leave. I look at the clock above my door, seeing that it reads 3:44 p.m., and know that in one minute my nurse is going to burst through the door like he has every day for the past eight days. I can't wait to get out of here.

Don't get me wrong, I like Jake. He knows how to start an IV so that it doesn't hurt, and he always grabs me extra pudding cups since the food here isn't filling. I just feel trapped is all. Jake is nice, but nice only gets you so far when most of what he talks to me about is medical related.

And don't even get me started on Marge. Her whole career has been nursing for forty-two years, and I swear this hospital must be trying to kick her out. She is a nice lady, but she can't poke an IV for the life of her.

On schedule, Jake pops in the door with three pudding cups and two spoons. But unlike most days here, he doesn't have a dinner menu in hand. I'll admit, part of me was concerned they wouldn't discharge me for one reason or another, but the fact that I'm not getting dinner assures me I can leave.

"Two pudding cups for you, one for me," Jake says, placing the desserts in front of me and then dragging a chair beside my bed. I lightly laugh at his repetitive nature. At least something can stay consistent.

"Thanks, Jake, really. For everything." When I dig into the cup, I relish in the soothing and delicious flavor of butterscotch, but I will be happy to never taste it again once I leave.

He mumbles something like, "you're welcome," eating his own . He can't stay long, that being a part of his routine, but Jake always sits and finishes his pudding with me.

When I finish my first cup, Jake looks at me and says, "Did your mom let you read the paper?" I give him a weird look, unsure as to what he means, but then he unfolds something from a pocket in his scrubs. I shake my head after reading it.

"I thought they weren't going to print it until Sunday," I say, as though that makes much more of a difference.

When I had finally been admitted into a room and out of the ICU, I was permitted visitors. Of course, my mom came right away, but the news and media outlets wanted in as well. After speaking with my mom, I decided I wasn't going to do any interviews without Brooke by my side.

Of course, I couldn't do that because the doctors wouldn't let me see her. They said Brooke had gotten pneumonia a day after we arrived at the hospital, and when I begged one of them to let me see her, I had a bit of an outburst.

Let's just say that one of the local news stations caught it on film and posted it online. Can't say I blame them. It got five million views overnight. Trauma equals money.

So, I did the interview, but only to set the record straight; I was tired of seeing outlets say untrue things about our accident, untrue things about Brooke and Andrew.

They agreed not to print the interview until after I spoke with Brooke, and when she got well enough to have visitors a week later, I was the first one in the door.

I was incredibly relieved to see her alive, and grinning at me. She was the only person I had seen who had been in the accident with me since we were admitted, and I was feeling all kinds of emotions being with her.

She hugged me very tight for someone recovering from a painful infection, and I cried hard. She told me that she saw the video, and she actually laughed. I laughed despite myself, and when I told her about the interview and what I had said, she was perfectly gracious.

Sometimes, her niceness is annoyingly adorable. This was further proven when she started to ask me how I was. How I really was.

I knew I couldn't lie to her, and I'm sure she knew it too. I told her everything: I was hurting, reeling from the pain of our rescue and the reality of what had happened to us. I was in agony that Andrew wasn't here with us and was instead in the ICU suffering worse injuries than the two of us. I told her that after the third day here, I had been psychoanalyzed and told I was experiencing shock, trauma, and grief. I wasn't shocked, and neither was she.

What I was surprised at was that she was taking everything a lot better than I expected. Her gentle state confused me, maybe because I had been poked at and prodded like a specimen for the past five days. Brooke stayed calm the entire time I sat with her, and I was there for as long as I could be. Jake even brought us pudding at 3:45 p.m.

In the few days we had been in the mountains, Brooke and I had depended on each other much more than we ever had before, and that brought us much closer. Before the accident, I was just a guy who pretty intensely liked this girl, and now I was having conversations with her like she is my best friend, because in a way she is. She is the only one who can truly understand how I felt in the mountains, because she was there for every moment.

When I had to leave to go back to my room, I caught the first glimpse of negative emotion in her eyes. The fear I had seen in her eyes that last day on the mountain. So, at my request, my mom had brought her old iPhones so that we could FaceTime all night. Both of us fell asleep, but neither of us ended the call when we woke up. The moment I could go back into her room, I was there, and the cycle continued. It felt good to have someone here who could relate to me, since Lucas and Andrew were at another hospital, and I think she felt similarly.

Today was different, though. Brooke hasn't been officially told she could leave today like we were hoping she could, and because I'm getting discharged, I can only be in her room for a short amount of time. Jake can't do me any favors when I'm not a patient.

Last night when she told me she had to wait until later today to find out if she could leave, I could see the pain on her face. She wants out of here just as badly as I do, if not more.

As Jake finishes his pudding cup and I'm finishing my second one, my phone gets a notification that Brooke is calling me. I open the FaceTime request and turn it toward Jake.

"Hi, Jake!" I hear Brooke say in a cheery tone.

"Hi, Ms. Brooke," Jake responds in a joking tone, only making her laugh a bit. "Well, I'll leave you two alone," Jake says when I turn the phone back towards me, and I wave goodbye to him, rolling my eyes when he puckers his lips to make fun of me.

"Guess what?" Brooke says, a smile on her face that I'm not expecting.

"The Beatles aren't actually dead, they're just vampires in hiding," I say, coming up with the most random thing I can think of. I just want to hear her laugh one more time.

"No, silly," she says, a giggle bubbling out of her. "I get to leave today!"

"Seriously?" I almost yell.

"Well, my doctor told me that as long as I have a place to stay nearby for a few days in case anything were to happen, he is fine with me leaving." I see the happiness on her face, and I know my own is reflecting the same emotion.

She is then silent for a moment, and I wonder what she is about to say. "I was going to ask your mom if you don't think she'd mind?" she adds in a meek tone. I know that my mom would be overjoyed to have Brooke in our house.

After I recovered and she met Brooke, she pulled me

aside and said that I had better snatch her up or someone else will. I rolled my eyes, but I secretly loved my mom's approval. Since that day, my mom has brought clothes, toiletries, and everything else that a person needs to Brooke. I think she is just excited to have someone Brooke's age that isn't a boy she can shower gifts on.

"You know my mother adores you. She'd do it in a heartbeat. Plus, she was going to have me extend an invitation to you since our house is close and you'd be around familiar faces." A thought occurs to me, and I add, "In fact, I'm going to text her right now and wait for her to say yes." I open my message app and type out a quick text outlining what Brooke had said to me.

Within seconds, my mother responds, *Of course! Brooke is welcome to stay with us and I will be happy to take care of her. You did tell her I invited her right?*

"See?" I say to Brooke. I screenshot my thread with my mom and send it to her. "Proof that you're in the running for my mother's favorite."

Brooke laughs again.

"It's good to hear you laugh," I say. "I feel like we've spent most of the time we have known each other being serious."

"I know," she says, her smile remaining, but it falters slightly. "I hate to put a damper on things, but have you heard any more about Lucas or Andrew?"

I sigh deeply. When we were airlifted out of Silverton, Andrew and Lucas had to be taken to Chesterton Hospital because of their severity. Everyone else was brought to Johnson Memorial.

It has been killing me knowing that there is nothing I can do for either Lucas or Andrew. Brooke has been trying to distract me while still allowing me to feel worried and scared for them. I told her recently that even though he is at another hospital, I could still feel him fighting tooth and nail to survive. She said it was a twin connection thing, and I was able to laugh, even though all I wanted to do was cry.

We still haven't heard of any major changes in Lucas or Andrew's cases. My mom has tried to relay what she has heard, but since they are both in the ICU with comas, we don't expect any major changes soon. The doctors tell us to be hopeful that they'll wake soon, but it isn't up to them when.

My mom was splitting her time between hospitals and being home with my sisters, but now that I am awake, I told her to check with Andrew more frequently than me. I know she would beat herself up if she missed him waking up. She has tried to be near him as much as possible with his doctors not allowing visitors in his room.

Because we have been separated at two different hospitals, the only updates I really receive are from my mom and Lydia. Today, though, since my mom is at home preparing my room—and probably one for Brooke—if we hear anything, it will be from Lydia.

"I haven't heard anything new today," Brooke says, interrupting my thoughts. "Lydia is over at Chesterton checking on Lucas, so if she hears anything, she'll probably text me." Lydia had gotten a phone from Target for cheap to use until she got a new phone, and she had been communicating with me through that to give me updates my mom couldn't.

"What time do you get discharged?" I ask, hoping to change the subject. Brooke notices but doesn't push me on it.

"What time do any of us get discharged? You know that getting discharged is a mess, right?"

"You know what I meant."

"Yeah, I do. As soon as your mom shows to pick you up, she just needs to sign a waiver for me and I'm good to go." I give her a thumbs up and send a quick text to my mom.

Oh, the good old days of getting to treat you like a child. I get to sign you out! My mother, ladies and gentlemen.

Then I remember something I had been meaning to ask Brooke when she first called.

"Hey Brooke, what did the psychiatrist say?" I ask her. Brooke had been nervous about meeting with her for reasons she couldn't quite explain herself.

"She told me that I was dealing with this extremely well under the circumstances. She said I likely have some PTSD, and maybe mild depression." She says the last part a bit quieter, as though she doesn't want to admit it. I don't push her, but wait for her to elaborate. "She thinks it is from before the accident, though. From everything that happened with my parents and my sister."

"Brooke, that's fair. You had to live through that, and you've been strong through it." I sigh, remembering when my psychoanalysis was over, I was given a list of treatment options that overwhelmed me.

I talked with my mom and Brooke about it, trying to work through the best option for me. There are lots of therapies to deal with traumas of all sorts, but when it came down to it, I decided to start with therapy.

"Have you decided what you want to do?" I ask, and she nods.

"Therapy two times a week, just like you," she says, leaning back in her bed.

Brooke then takes out the book my mom brought her yesterday per her request. She starts to read it out loud to me, and for the next hour I listen to her voice.

In the middle of Brooke's next sentence, my mom texts me, *Your rooms are set up and I'll be there in thirty minutes.* I relay the message to Brooke, and she continues to read.

I still get lost in her voice. It's just as soothing as it was in those woods.

After thirty minutes pass, Jake returns to my room to interrupt Brooke's reading.

"Your mom is here signing your papers. I heard something about her taking Ms. Brooke home with her as well?" he asks with a raised eyebrow. I laugh at him, but Brooke responds.

"Yes, sir. She is taking me with Jackson and her." She sounds so happy, and Jake grins at the two of us.

"Alright then. Jackson, you can head downstairs as soon as your mom finishes that paperwork, and Brooke, you can leave when you sign your last form. I'll bring it down to you right now." Jake leaves the room, and I can tell that from the way he holds the door open that my mom is about to walk in.

Sure enough, my mom jumps into the room, acting as though I never would have suspected her, and says, "Surprise!

Did you miss me?"

I am happy to see her, but slightly embarrassed at my mother.

"Of course, he did, Ms. Carter," Brooke says, giving me a goofy look. I stick my tongue out at her in a playful gesture and respond to her.

"Okay, enough of that. I'll see you in a few," I say in a playful banter.

She laughs at me, knowing I'm joking from the grin on my face. "Sure, sure. You hate me."

"Of course. Go away now."

"See you in two minutes." She ends the call, and my mom shakes her head.

"What?" I ask.

"You'll understand sometime soon," she responds cryptically.

"Thanks, Mom," I retort, unsure of what she means. "Let's go."

I get out of my bed, already dressed and ready to go since I was technically discharged an hour ago and Marge had removed my IV's while Brooke was reading to me. I grab my backpack, and we head down the hallway to where the elevators are. We ride the elevator to the seventh floor, and I walk to the familiar room.

When I reach the door, I knock and then open it slowly, saying, "Decent?"

When she responds, "Yep," I swing the door open and maneuver around her bed to hug her. She is already standing, so when I grab her, she is lifted a little off the floor.

"Go away," I whisper into her hair playfully.

"You're the one hugging me!" She giggles, a melodic sound bubbling out of her.

"You just won't leave me alone. Why do you have to be so mean?" I ask her, only hugging her tighter.

It feels good to have her body against mine. It assures me that this is real. I'm not dreaming. We are alive, and she is safe. It also, just for a minute, separates us from the reality that is my brother and Lucas are still not awake yet.

When I pull away, she turns to me with a look in her eyes I can't quite place. Then she glances behind me at my mom.

"Hi, Ms. Carter! Thank you so much for agreeing to help me," she says, but my mom immediately shuts her down.

"Brooke, honey, anything. Anything at all. Don't worry about it at all." My mom is the genuinely one of the kindest humans.

Brooke says, "Alright, we're ready then."

My mom leads the way to the car while Brooke stays next to me, clinging to my arm loosely, but firmly. Maybe it is to keep her standing, or maybe she just wants to feel the familiarity, but whatever it is, I'm grateful for it.

When we reach the car, I know neither of us particularly want to sit in the back seat, but I force Brooke to sit in the front passenger's seat. I am, I remind her, a gentleman. She finally gives in after fighting me and takes the front.

We sit for a moment, my mom trying to make us feel as comfortable as possible. I can feel the anxiousness in the way my stomach churns, and my chest is tightening from just sitting in the car. I know I can get over it by breathing slowly and trying to relax, but it isn't easy.

I look at Brooke through the rearview mirror, making sure she is okay, and she looks back at me assuredly. After ten minutes of my mom reminding us that she will be extremely careful, she finally starts the engine of her car.

As we drive away, I look at the horizon in front of us, reminded of the view from the clearing. Then I look at Brooke in front of me, staring out the window.

We're here. We're alive.

Chapter 4
Before

Wind bites harshly and painfully on my skin through what I can only assume are the broken windshields and windows. It feels like knives stabbing over and over, and part of me wonders if I really am being repeatedly stabbed. The biting cold sends shivers across my body and my ears are flooded with the howling of the wind.

My eyes flutter open, and for a moment, I have forgotten where I am. And in an instant, it all rushes back to me, startling my eyes wide open.

I'm alive. *How am I alive?*

My ribs are badly bruised and the fact that I blacked out combined with the massive pain in my head indicates I have a concussion. Hopefully it's not too severe. I know there is glass sticking into the skin on my neck, so I pull what I can feel out and pray no one else is as badly injured—or worse.

The others. Brooke is still hugged against me, and I have to strain to move her enough to make sure she is breathing. *One. Two. A breath.* I let out a sigh of relief knowing that whatever happened, I protected her.

I look around at everyone else, and I see that Andrew isn't moving, though neither is anyone else. My heart starts to pound. *Is he dead?* I focus all my gaze onto his chest, and when I see it rise an inch, I let out a huge sigh. At least I know he is alive. Then, I look around at everyone else, seeing that no one else is responsive yet. Carefully, I lean Brooke against the seat, moving slowly because of the massive pain all of my muscles are in. Still, my brain is yelling to move faster.

I open the car door carefully, because I don't know how we survived, but I know the car wasn't crushed from the impact, which means we got stuck against or in something. That might have saved our lives. Looking below the door now ajar I see the car cannot be more than eight feet off the ground, stuck in the branches of a tree. I also look around for the car that hit us, wondering where it is, but I can't see it from where we are.

Eight feet is still quite a way to drop, though not compared to the drop we had earlier. If I try to get out of the car, my movements might cause it to fall. I have to be careful. I look over Brooke to Lydia. She has a gash above her eyebrow, but it doesn't look that deep. But her arm—it's obviously broken from the bend in the middle of her arm.

Silently, I pray for nothing to go wrong as I maneuver around Brooke, sliding her to where I was sitting, and check on Lydia. I carefully move her blonde hair to the side to see if I was right about the cut. I was, but it's still bleeding too much, so I look around for something that might work well to stop the bleeding. My eyes land on Lucas and the bandana around his tanned neck. *Perfect.*

I lean over and untie the bandana from around his neck and fold it so that the thickness will stunt the bleeding. Then I wrap it like a headband, under the back of her head and her hair, tying it over the wound like I was taught in CPR training. Then I look at her arm.

It's not good. There are at least two breaks, and while I don't know a lot about medicine, I figure based on the breaks combined with the bruising on her arm, it will probably require surgery.

"She needs to be set, splinted and given a sling," says a faint voice from over my shoulder. Eyes wide, I turn to face Brooke, glad she is alive, but saddened over the pain in her voice.

"Are you alright? I checked on you a few minutes ago but you didn't have anything visibly wrong."

She nods, closing her eyes and then reopening them. "I think your hug worked. I probably only have a mild concussion from whiplash." My heart swells, knowing I did something to help her. If only I could have done the same for everyone else in the car.

She moves slowly, but leans over, despite my assurance that I can handle this. "I have a T-shirt in my backpack. It was on the floor. Can you find it?" I'm confused because right now doesn't seem like the time to be changing clothes, but she continues. "I'm going to use it to make her a sling."

I lean down carefully, realizing I haven't told her how far we are from the ground and how intentionally we have to move.

After a few moments, I see the blue backpack with the white flowers that she insisted ride with her and not in the trunk. The zipper compartment is still halfway open, but with one tug, I can see the shirt is underneath her *Wuthering Heights* book.

I hand Brooke the shirt and watch as she carefully wraps Lydia's arm. It seems like she has done this before from the care she takes. Then I look at my brother and his best friend, a mistake.

Andrew seems to be okay, but I really can't tell from this angle. Lucas, on the other hand, has a gash that stretches from his temple to his eye, clearly in need of stitches, and his arm is also broken lower on his arm, near his wrist.

Brooke, in wrapping Lydia's arm, must have awoken her because she gasps for air, her eyes popped open. Her cries are painful to hear, but what concerns me is that she is thrashing around. I look at Brooke, silently confirming the worry on her face.

"Lydia, honey," Brooke says in a calming voice. "I am so sorry, but you can't move around like that. You can scream as loud as you want—you basically shattered your radius, after all—but you can't move. We're still not on the ground, so if we move too suddenly, the car might fall."

Lydia's eyes go wide, but something in them shows she understands. When Brooke finishes wrapping her arm, I look to my brother and his friend and turn back to her.

"How are we going to get to them? Lucas clearly needs medical attention, and I'm not sure what Andrew needs." I sigh, and Brooke shakes her head.

"I don't know. How far did the drop look to you? If we

can get out of the car, it's probably for the better. Maybe we can get help," she says hopefully, but we both know that there weren't any cars behind us when we were hit, so the likelihood of someone seeing us go over the mountainside was close to none.

"I don't really know. Eight feet is a low assumption, but even that high of a drop could break our legs," I say. Lydia's eyes are bulging out of her head and I'm wondering if I should not have shared that information with her.

"Okay," Brooke says shakily. "Then I need to look Lucas over. That injury on his head might be life threatening."

I look around, unsure of how she will get to the front without sending the car toppling the rest of the way down.

"Brooke, be careful," Lydia and I say at the same time, and she looks back at us. She then starts to slowly climb toward the front, stepping over the center console.

"Grab my hand and lean backwards into the rear of the car. I'm lighter than you so the weight displacement won't be too great," she says.

I lean back and grab her hand as she situates herself in front of Lucas, taking my hand in her right and using her left to move his jet-black hair out of the way. From the way she winces, I know that it's bad.

"He's going to need more than a few stitches," Brooke says. "If we were back home, I'd be rushing him to a hospital. If he doesn't wake up soon, I don't know if he is going to make it."

I sigh in frustration. "Okay. What about Andrew?"

She looks toward him, my hand still grasping hers. "I don't see any visible injury. It's possible he may have internal bleeding, but I would have to check for bruising. Switch hands, please." She looks pointedly at our clasped hands, and I lean my left hand down toward her. She takes it, switching hands, and then leans over to check on Andrew. She lifts his shirt to see if any bruising is there, but after she looks over him thoroughly, she doesn't seem to find any.

"I would check for brain activity if I had a light. Do you have a flashlight?" she asks me.

I shake my head, regretting not having thought to have brought one for our trip. "But I do have a flashlight on my phone." I reach for my phone in my back pocket with my free hand, only to see it is smashed. I show her my screen, a defeated look showing on my face.

"Do you know where my phone is?" she asks. I look around the bottom of the car, but I can't see her phone. I assume it's smashed too, even if we were to find it. I look to Lydia, silently hoping she has her phone, and it is free of a single crack. She shakes her head.

"It's okay," Brooke says. "I'm sure we'll be rescued soon, and they can check for us. I'm going to come back there now, okay?" I stretch both of my arms to her in attempt to pull her back, but the moment she starts to move, so does the car.

It's a low creaking noise, one that I never wanted to hear. All three of our eyes are wide, and I know that no matter what happens, if this car is going to nosedive, it will crush Brooke. Quickly, I tug her to me over the center console and look to Lydia.

"Hold on. We are going to fall," I say, trying to keep any wavering out of my voice.

The car creaks again, this time much louder, and we start to lean. I lean Brooke and I to the side behind the front passenger's seat, hoping to protect us a bit more. As the car creaks forward, I feel the wind start to pick up, biting more and more against my skin and my face. Then comes the weightless feeling when we fell the first time. I close my eyes and wait.

One second.

Two seconds.

Three seconds.

Crash.

We land hard on the ground, and the noise of broken glass and creaking metal stings my ears. I'm slammed against the roof of the car, and then, silence.

I open my eyes slowly and look around. We landed upside down, but by some miracle, the hood hadn't caved in, probably because of the rack on top of the car. The front windshield isn't broken, but judging from the cold breeze on my neck, the back one is. I look at Brooke to make sure she's okay, and she nods in response. I look over at Lydia and see that she is shaken, holding in the pain of her arm, but also okay.

Then, a guttural scream from the front seat. It's Andrew, and the front of the car is crushing his legs. Quickly, Brooke and I look at each other, nodding in agreement, and I open the door.

When I was slammed against the ceiling, the top of the car became the bottom. Where Brooke and I are now slanted in the car, I have to open the door backwards and climb out carefully, helping her out as well.

We quickly maneuver our way around the car to get to the

driver's seat where Andrew is screaming.

I wrench the crushed-in door open and look at my brother's legs. Only one of them is pinned beneath the front of the car, the other somehow unscathed.

Brooke looks at me and says, "You need to figure out how to get his leg out of there. I'm going to check him over."

I nod, trying to figure out how I am going to move crushed metal. I need something that will lift it off him, like a crowbar or something.

Or a car jack. That would work, and as I move to get to the trunk, I pray my twin is as prepared for a flat tire as he is for his exams. The window to the trunk is shattered, and as I try to open the door, it doesn't budge. I use as much force as I can, placing a foot against the fender and pull.

After a minute or two, the SUV's trunk finally budges, and I see that my snowboard and some of our bags are missing. The ones that are left are covered in shards of glass, falling out of the car. I unroll the arm of my flannel and try to brush most of it away so that when I move the bags, I don't cut myself. The snow is making the bottom of my pants drenched, making my legs underneath subject to the cold. A shiver runs up my spine, and I wonder how cold it must be. Thankfully, Lucas had his jacket up front with him from our gas station pit-stop, and both Lydia and Brooke's were still in here as well.

Andrew's screams have stopped by now, and once I have all the bags out of the car, I undo the floor of the trunk to reveal the spare tire and the tools I was praying would be there. I quickly grab the car jack and its lever, closing the floor and return to the bags. I end up putting most of the bags back into the trunk, awkwardly since the car is upside down now, and walk back to the front of the car. Then I grab the small machine and jam it under the crushed metal.

I pump the lever up and down about seven times. On the first three, I didn't hear anything, but on the fourth, the metal makes a small screech. By the seventh, I can see the metal has left his leg, and Brooke is quickly, but gently pushing me to the side to check him.

"He was fine when I checked his eyes, and he didn't have any bruises so he should be okay. The leg, however, looks crushed. I'd be surprised if he could limp on it." She looks back at me now, meeting my eyes. "I'm going to need another shirt to wrap his leg. Maybe two?"

I return to the luggage and open his bag. A jacket and a plethora of T-shirts meet my gaze. I grab two of them and then run them to Brooke, watching as she wraps his leg, just as caring as she was with Lydia. Andrew is even able to huskily thank her, a crack in his voice from the pain, I'm sure. Then she looks over to where Lucas is sitting and coming to silently. I gesture toward him with my head, looking directly at her.

We both make our way to the right side of the car to check on Lucas. This time, Lydia joins us. She is clearly still in shock, but doesn't want to be alone, and I don't blame her.

"Hey, Lucas," Brooke says softly. "How are you feeling?"

He laughs a little, clearly in pain from doing so. "I feel like I just got hit by a car and fell down the side of a mountain," he says.

"Twice," Lydia quietly adds.

Lucas's face pales when she adds this, but by this point

Brooke is checking him to see if he is okay and he becomes distracted. I stay back and watch. Brooke acts like she has done this most of her life.

"Hey, Lydia, can you do me a favor?" Brooke asks. "Lucas here is going to need a bandage for his head and a shirt for his arm. Knowing this guy, he brought some extra bandanas. Would you mind going to look for one or two?"

As Lydia leaves, Brooke pulls me to the side, out of earshot for Lucas.

"He's stable for now, but I don't have a light so I can't see how his head is. I can tell you that I'm shocked he woke up. I can't imagine, though, that he doesn't have some kind of internal bleeding, and his arm is in terrible condition. I'm going to try to wrap it with another shirt to keep it from getting infected, but it will be hard. He needs a doctor, and I can't do a lot here."

"So, what are we going to do?" I ask her.

"Well, we're going to need to make a fire. The light is already fading so quickly; it'll be gone soon. Do you know how to do that?"

I inwardly I chuckle, knowing she didn't know I was a Boy Scout.

"Yeah, I was a Boy Scout so I know a thing or two. Can you think of anything else?"

I see a slight grin appear on her face, but then she looks past me, and I turn to see Lydia returning with a shirt in her good hand.

"I think his bag might be missing, but I found a shirt in Andrew's bag that you might be able to use," she says, holding it up. Brooke thanks her and goes to wrap Lucas's head. I follow, with Lydia going to Andrew's side.

"We can't sleep upside down," I say, "and Lucas needs to be moved to a better position. What should we do?" I look at the car, flipped upside down, and try to think. The seats aren't going to move easily, but there is a chance I could rip the material to lay on the floor at minimum.

Brooke must see the wheels in my head turning because she asks, "What do you need?"

"Something sharp," I mutter under my breath. I see out of the corner of my eye that Brooke is also thinking, and then her face lights up.

"What about the glass? There have to be some pieces that we can wrap, right?" she says. I hope that will be enough. Near the broken windshield I see a large piece of glass and find one that will work and use the sleeve of my flannel to pick it up before walking to the car door I left open.

Looking at all five seats, I notice that the front seats I might be able to remove from the car if I figure it out. It takes a good half hour to remove everything safely, but when I do, I look at the finished product with pride. It isn't pretty, but it will work. The floor has been turned into a padded area, with the insulation below the seat covering, and it is spacious enough that we will be able to fit if we squeeze tight. We will still be cold, but at least we won't be dead. If it weren't for the fact that the normal Colorado winter storms weren't for another week, we'd be in a worse place.

Then I look at the front seats. I know that if I move them forward and wrench it correctly, the seats will pop out at some point. I look over at Brooke, who has been watching me with her arms around her stomach, and gesture to Lucas with my head.

"I need to move him if I am going to move the seats. Andrew too."

She nods, letting me know it will be safe enough to do so. I open the front door and look at Lucas.

"Do what you got to, do but don't you dare hold this over me," he says jokingly.

"Don't worry," I say as I lift him bridal style. "I won't tell anyone about our special time together." After I set Lucas in the snow, I go to Andrew's side, helping him outside of the car this time instead of lifting him.

Then I return to the car, moving the seat forward and back, trying to use any kind of leverage I can. When I finish the right side, I look over at the driver's seat, knowing the process is going to be brutal again.

I complete my work with more bruising on my back, and I'm feeling the pain in my chest even more. But I'm proud of my work. I can also see that, as Brooke and I help Lucas and Andrew into their new seats, she is extremely thankful. I shut the doors as I let them relax now, and she turns to me.

"Thank you for that. I'm not sure what we would have done," she says.

"It wasn't any problem," I say, rubbing my hands. I wince since they are raw from the labor. Looking at them closely, I can see they are torn up, not bleeding, but the cold isn't helping the pain.

"Look, Jackson," Brooke says. "The fall we took was deep.

Looking around, I think it's quite unlikely we're going to be spotted all the way down here. The only way anyone saw us go down was if the other car told someone, and I think if that were true a team of some sorts would be here. I haven't seen the other car yet, have you?"

I shake my head.

"Nobody is here to save us," Brooke continues, "and we don't know how long we're going to be here. Hopefully the other car is still up there, but for the meantime, we need to stay safe and warm tonight."

Then I see her looking at my neck. I had forgotten it had glass in it earlier, and when I removed it, a cut remained.

"That doesn't look too deep. Can I help?" she asks me, and I nod. She takes her hand and carefully pulls the remainder of shattered glass out. Since I had gotten the majority out earlier, there wasn't much left, and thankfully she was right—it's not that deep. I have a little bit of bleeding, but not much.

"I'm done," she says softly.

"Alright. I'm going to look for wood and moss for the fire. You and Lydia need to grab your coats from the trunk and help Lucas into his. Andrew's is in his bag," I say.

I can't see the road we fell from, and not just because it's getting darker. The snow makes anything over one hundred feet away slightly blurry and anything farther away is almost completely obscured. I start to look around the car for some dry wood or anything that will keep the fire burning until I see some brush that is hidden under some rocks that seem dry enough to be a good base.

I pick enough for the fire tonight and stand up, turning to

go back to the car when something catches my eye. The car that hit us is lying a few feet away. I had assumed, at some point, that the car hadn't gone over the cliff, so seeing it now causes any hope that I had for rescue to leave my stomach cramping in fear.

Since the people hadn't yet tried to find us, I worry the worst has happened. After a moment of debate—do I go over there alone or get some help—I decide to talk to the group first. I walk over and lay my materials near the car before tapping Brooke on the shoulder, interrupting her checking on Andrew once more. I notice that she is wearing her jacket, and I look over at Lydia who is also wearing hers. At least I don't have to worry as much in terms of that.

"The car that hit us is over there," I point in the direction I saw the car.

At this point, Andrew is acting like nothing is wrong with him, and so it doesn't surprise me when the words, "Let's go check it out," leave his mouth.

"No," I say sternly. "Brooke and I can go check it out. Or I will if she thinks she needs to stay with you, but you are not well enough to move yet."

I had made the mistake of pointing to where the car is, though, and Andrew has already grabbed a large branch from the ground and is using it as a walking stick, limping toward the car before I can stop him. My twin may be two minutes older than me, but sometimes, he acts as though he is twenty years older. I follow behind him, shaking my head in disapproval, and Brooke follows me.

"I agree he shouldn't be walking on his leg," Brooke says,

"but I can't exactly tackle him. If he feels well enough to walk, maybe it just looks worse than it is."

"Yeah, but he is my brother. I don't want him to hurt himself any more than he already is."

"And you think that if he was any worse, he wouldn't still walk over there? He isn't my brother and I know he would do that with certainty."

I know she is right, but wishing she wasn't.

As we near the car, I see Andrew has disappeared. I frown, confused, until his body pulls out of the back of the car. Not just him, though—a little girl, who can't be more than seven years old. He has her in his arms, and she is clinging to him like he is protecting her from something. I use my head to gesture to the rest of the car, knowing she wouldn't be here without her parents. He shakes his head, a look in his eyes that pierces right into my stomach, and Brooke turns around.

At first, I didn't know what the lumps of snow through the shattered windshield are—but when I see the look in his eyes, I know. They're bodies, dead bodies. The little girl in my brother's arms is the sole survivor of the car in front of me.

I am overwhelmed with a sick feeling in my gut. I know I couldn't have done anything, but seeing this little girl with no one breaks my heart. I look at my brother, feeling fortunate to even be seeing him now. While the other car was at fault, I can see the guilt evident on Andrew's face.

I turn around, putting my arm around Brooke. I expected her to be heaving or crying, but instead, she takes a few deep breaths and looks at me before walking over to Andrew.

He tries to pass the little girl to Brooke, but she whimpers and holds tighter to him, so he shakes his head indicating he is going to walk her back to camp.

I look at the car again, feeling my stomach churn at the thought of the girl in my brother's arms being in forced proximity with, likely, her family members who are no longer alive. I look back at Brooke who is following Andrew and join her, shaking my head to try to clear it.

As we're walking, Brooke says to me, "Do you have enough to start a fire for tonight?"

"Yes, I found what I need, although a match would be great."

"Thought you'd say that," my brother says from ahead of me. "I was able to grab a lighter from the cupholder before grabbing her," he says, gesturing to the little girl, whose head is now on his shoulder.

Brooke turns to me and says, "What are we going to do with her?"

The truth is, it doesn't surprise me that Andrew is the one she wants. Growing up, my dad wasn't ever in the picture, but my two younger sisters needed some semblance of a dad, so Andrew and I always stepped in. But even then, I always felt like Andrew was better at it than I was.

"I don't know. But even if she doesn't leave his side, she'll be okay. He's great with kids."

"What are we going to do about," she pauses. "Them." She doesn't need to point. I know she is referring to the owners of the other car.

"I'm not sure there is much we can do. I guess we could bury them, but I have a feeling they'll just be dug up. I think it might be better to leave them." I feel sick even saying that. "Am I a horrible person for even voicing that?" I ask rhetorically.

"No," Brooke says. "Just realistic."

We reach our now "camp," and I go to where I left the fire materials. Brooke walks over with Andrew and the little girl to the car and helps them both sit down in the back.

I pick up the materials and start building the base for the fire, clearing an area where snow isn't deep and placing a lot of leaves there. Then I put the base on top of the leaves, turning as I feel someone watching me.

"Sorry," Brooke says. "I didn't mean to scare you. I chuckle.

"You didn't. Just startled me. Did you bring the lighter?"

She hands it to me. I try it a few times before it produces a flame that can light the brush. It catches fire slowly, but then starts burning brightly. I put some other wood I grabbed earlier that was too wet next to the fire, hoping the fire dries it so we won't have to worry about that later. The fire is close enough to the car that we might have a chance at being just a little warmer, but not that much.

"Well, at least we can stay a little warmer now," Brooke says. "Thank you, Jackson."

"Don't thank me. Andrew found the lighter—"

"No, I mean thank you. For staying calm today and helping me. I know that I was panicking, so I'm sure you were too. We are okay for now, so thank you."

I shake my head in disbelief. "Brooke, you were the reason it was easier to stay calm. Yeah, I was freaking out on the inside, but you took care of everyone. I should be thanking you."

She laughs. "Well, we can't just spend the night thanking

each other. Come on, let's find a way to get some sleep." She offers me a hand to stand up, and I take it. We walk a few steps to the car and look inside. Andrew is half-asleep with the little girl clinging to him. Lydia and Lucas had passed out too. I guess we will have to tell them the news when we wake up.

I grab a couple of the towels we brought just in case from another bag. On each of the doors, I open it enough to slip the towel in and cover the window, hopefully keeping the snow out for the night.

Brooke climbs in first and grabs her backpack to use as a pillow. She situates herself and I climb in as well, but not before taking off my flannel and handing it to her. It is thick and fleece lined, so I know that it will be more comfortable and warmer to wear.

"This is going to be more comfortable than that backpack," I say. "And before you say anything about me being cold, I'm closer to the fire and I have a towel as a blanket. Take it, please and thank you."

She rolls her eyes, but I can tell she is grateful. I adjust my headrest to be more comfortable to sleep in, and finally feel the tiredness in my body. It's easy to give in, and right before I completely drift off, I hear a soft, "Thank you."

Chapter 5
After

As we pull into my mom's driveway, a funny feeling washes over me. This place feels more like a distant memory than where I grew up; I was just here for Thanksgiving, but already it feels like a foreign place.

I step out of the car, letting the coolness of the air meet my skin. It doesn't bite or sting, yet it hurts in a different way. It's like a painful memory.

I open the passenger's side door for Brooke and offer my hand to her. She takes it with a, "thank you," and clutches her small gym bag as she gets out.

When my mom was finally able to see me in the hospital, she had brought me some clothes, a toothbrush and toothpaste, and her old phone, since our luggage has still not been recovered. Not that I wanted to wear any of that clothing anyway.

My mom had purchased Brooke a T-shirt and sweatpants and a few other items from a local store and brought them to me in a little gym bag to give to her when she got over her pneumonia. At first, Brooke didn't want to accept the clothing, but my mom made it a point to let her know that clothing is a basic necessity, and it really wasn't a big deal. Finally, she accepted the gift, profusely thanking her.

I can tell that Brooke isn't used to having people do things for her like that, since her family isn't around. I think she finally feels more comfortable with my mom, since all the gifts and niceties are just who my mom is.

As we walk toward the door to the house, I feel a pit in my stomach, knowing I'm here and Andrew isn't. My mom gestures toward the door, indicating that it is open, but before I can even turn the doorknob, two small humans attack me with hugs. I'm a bit startled at first as they run at me, arms open wide, but as soon as I realize it is Maggie and Kayla, I breathe deeply and feel the familiarity wash over me.

Kayla still isn't tall enough to reach my torso yet, so I bend down to pick her up. She stuffs her head into my neck, and I know she's crying from the shaking of her body. Maggie, being twelve, is hugging me around my waist. I don't feel embarrassed at their display of emotion around me, I never have, but I am conscious that Brooke is here with us.

I look at her and mouth *sorry,* but she just shakes her head as if to assure me she is fine. Still, I can see her eyes are filling with tears, and I know it's because she's thinking about her own sister. I remember the vulnerability Brooke had when she told me about her family on the mountain, and I know it is a painful topic. Right now, all I want to do is hug her and never let go. I look at my mom, seeing she has tears brimming at the corners of her eyes.

I pull away from Maggie, nudging my nose against Kayla's, and say, "I missed you two so much." My voice cracks, and I can't help but feel the emotion wash over me. I will never forget how I felt on that mountain, how I thought I would never see them again. The pain that caused me—I can't ever forget it. I also can't look at either of them without thinking how wrong it is that Andrew isn't here too.

Maggie can't open her mouth without crying, even though she never cries in front of Mom. I place a finger under her chin, tilting her head to look at mine and say, "Why don't we go inside so we don't make the house too cold and I'll fix you some hot chocolate?"

This makes her beam, and I know she is remembering how last Christmas I almost drank my weight in hot chocolate.

Maggie goes inside while I put Kayla down. I hold the door for Brooke and my mom to enter first.

I close the door behind me, a warmth enveloping me that I now can't ever take for granted. My mom's house is always warm, even in the Colorado winter, because she can't stand to be cold. She has the highest electricity bill in the neighborhood, but she doesn't care. As long as she stays warm.

I look over at Brooke, who has a slightly uncomfortable look on her face. My sisters are looking at her curiously, but they don't say anything. I think they are more surprised than anything, but I had assumed Mom had told them Brooke was coming home with us.

Then, out of nowhere, Kayla asks, "Are you Jackson's girlfriend?"

My face burns from embarrassment, but Brooke's is only sporting an embarrassed grin.

"Kayla, you haven't even been introduced to Brooke and that is what you ask her?" I say, shaking my head.

"Jackson and I are really good friends. Do you have a best friend, Kayla?" Brooke asks, kneeling slightly to look Kayla in the eyes.

"My bestest friend is Halle. She is in my class, and she likes horses. Her mom told me that this summer we're going to go ride horses because her family owns a ranch." Kayla babbles on, which only makes Brooke grin wider.

"Well Jackson and I are bestest friends, aren't we, Jackson?" She turns to face me, and all I want to say to her is, "We're more than that." Being attached at the hip these past two weeks has done nothing to stop my feelings for Brooke, but we haven't decided anything. I want to believe that her closeness to me those days on the mountain was her feelings for me developing, but I think she has just become comfortable with me.

Still, I turn to Kayla and say, "Yeah, we are the bestest of friends." It can't be that true, of course, since we have only been acquaintances for a year or so and friends for even less time, but after the mountain, I feel like Brooke and I have lived a whole life together.

My mom clears her throat and says, "Well, I was promised a cup of hot chocolate, and I would like to collect it. How about you girls?"

All the girls nod enthusiastically.

"If I must," I say, trying not to laugh. As I grab the powder and milk in the kitchen, I recognize that the upset feeling I had experienced when pulling into the driveway had not left my stomach, still causing an ache to know that this joking manner I am putting on was usually Andrew's persona. I feel like I am just acting a part I was never meant to play.

To distract myself, I decided to run up to my room to grab some music. I have an old cassette player with some tapes that are fun to listen to while baking—I used to it a lot as a kid. When I walk downstairs, my mom laughs when she sees the tapes in my hand, and Brooke looks over to me, glancing at the tapes.

"You have a cassette player?" she asks.

"I know, I know, but I'm old-school. I used to listen to these all the time growing up." She grins at me when I say this, and as I put in the tape and the music starts to play softly in the background, I start to make the hot chocolate.

Brooke sits down at the counter, watching me as I continue to make the chocolate beverage. I meet her eyes and she sticks her tongue out at me, playfully. I shake my head, trying not to laugh, and in return I contort my face. Immediately, she laughs, and I feel my heart jump a little.

I pour the milk into a pan, heating it up, and when it is ready, I add the powder. As I stir it, I hear my sisters, who have left the room, laughing upstairs. I close my eyes for a moment, listening and remembering all those times when we were younger, and I would think it was the best sound on the earth.

I feel myself grinning, and when I open my eyes, I spoon a little of the drink to try. It's ready, so I grab five glasses and ladle enough for each person to have some. There is plenty left in the pan, so I cover it before yelling for my sisters to come down. Then I pause the music, setting the player aside so it doesn't get damaged.

My mom walks into the room and says, "I missed that. You, yelling for Andrew or Maggie and Kayla to get downstairs for breakfast or to get to school. Seeing them around you, it reminds me how much I miss you boys when you're gone."

I miss it too, even just being here with my family. I knew it would be hard leaving for college, but I talked with Maggie and Kayla before Andrew and I left to explain that I was going to be back all the time. With my games and practice, it hasn't been easy to keep that promise though, and I can't help but feel guilt start to fill my stomach.

Footsteps thunder down the stairs and both of my sisters rush into the room. I hand everyone a cup, keeping one for myself, and go sit down next to Brooke.

The chocolate is good, and it's warm, but the best part about it is being with my family. The only thing that would make it better is if Andrew were here with us. I know that my being back probably calms a small part of my mom's heart from bursting in pain, but Andrew is still too severely injured to come home.

I sit here thinking about my brother as my sisters and Brooke converse. I can feel the eyes on me, but I don't speak. I'm happy to be home, but the pit in my stomach is coming back, more painful than ever.

I excuse myself to the restroom, but when I close the door behind me, I turn on the faucet and bend over the sink, closing my eyes. I start to feel the tears fall, feeling the lump in my throat try to force its way up. I instead choke on a sob, but I don't force it to go down.

A slight knock raps on the door and I turn off the faucet. I wipe my face with a tissue then open the door slightly, expecting to see my mom. Instead, I am met with those piercing blue eyes, filled with concern.

"Are you okay?" she asks me, and I shake my head. I lean back against the sink, my back to the mirror, and Brooke comes into the bathroom, closing the door behind her. Her body slants against the wall across from me, close enough that our feet almost touch.

"What's going on? You were just so happy a few moments ago," she asks me.

"It doesn't feel right, being here without Andrew, I mean." I blow air out of my mouth harshly before continuing. "I just feel like I'm an actor in a part I was never supposed to be given. This was all Andrew, taking care of the girls, making them happy. I don't want to try to replace him, or even think I could, especially when he might wake up soon." I feel a tear fall down my face, and Brooke wipes it away.

"No one thinks you're trying to replace him. No one can replace him. I think they are all just happy to have you back. They thought they lost you—I thought I lost you in that cabin. I'm not them, but I can bet that having you back is better than having no one back." She sighs before continuing. "Your mom just got a call from the hospital. Nothing new, but they did tell her that Andrew can have some visitors now. She wants to head over but asked me to ask you if you wanted to come with her."

It isn't a question, of course, since I would say yes, a thousand times, but I nod.

"If you'll come with me," I say, my voice shaking slightly.

"Of course I will, if you want me there."

"I need you there."

She smiles softly and wipes another tear off my face. "For the record, you're so much stronger than I am. If he was my twin, I would be taking this a lot harder than you. You're grounding your family right now, though. You're grounding me. Don't feel like you shouldn't be here. I'm grateful you're here, and so is your family."

I return her smile, trying to ignore how my heart is palpitating.

She moves to the door, opening it and leaving it open behind her. I follow her back to the kitchen. My sisters are watching something on the TV in the living room and my mom tells Maggie to watch Kayla for a little while.

She looks at Brooke and I and asks, "Ready?"

When we get in the car, we begin the drive. The hospital Brooke and I were in is thirty minutes northwest, but the hospital Lucas and Andrew are at is equidistant northeast.

I listen to the hum of the wheels on the pavement to try to focus on anything other than the fact that I'm in a car on a highway right now. The anxiety doesn't stop and the drive feels like it takes forever, even though we make it without any traffic. When we finally pull into the first floor of the parking garage, I almost rush out of the car. The door closes behind me, and I reach forward to open Brooke's door for her. The same smile from earlier stretches across her face. My heart jumps knowing that I caused that, and when she shakes her head laughing slightly, I almost wonder if she could hear my thoughts.

We go to the hospital's entrance, and the whole time my hand is clutching Brooke's tightly. I'm scared for what I'm going to find, but I need to see him. My heart hurts to be away from Andrew, to not hear him laughing at me and making jokes about being the older twin.

I start to pace back and forth while my mom checks us in. Brooke notices and grabs my hand again, squeezing it until I look at her.

"Breathe," she says. "It's alright. You're going to see him and it's alright."

I know she's right, of course, and yet I can't seem to calm myself down.

We walk to the elevator, riding it to the fifteenth floor, and when the doors open, I follow my mom down a long hallway to room fifteen thirty-two. I stand outside the door, Brooke's hand still clutching mine. She gives me a squeeze once more, as if to say it's alright and I can open the door. So, I do.

My brother is hooked up to a bunch of tubes, wires, and other medical equipment that I don't know the names of. If it weren't him, I would wonder if the person would make it. But he is my brother. I can't think like that. He wouldn't want me to think like that.

We walk farther into the room, seeing that there is a reclining chair for someone to sit in. I drop Brooke's hand, walking toward Andrew's bed now, and stop next to him, beckoning my mom to sit down in the chair. She shakes her head, eyes filling with tears. I've always hated seeing my mom cry. She continues to stare at my brother, a hand over her mouth and tears starting to fall down her face.

She doesn't deserve this. He doesn't deserve this.

I look at my brother, lying helpless in his hospital bed. His leg is elevated with about twenty poles extending around his knee in a cage-like design. His hands are wrapped slightly because of the frostbite recovery.

He looks anything but fashionable, yet I know my brother would turn to me right now if he could and say, *"It's the new trend. How do you like it?"* And I would laugh. And it would all be okay.

It would be. It isn't. I look away from my brother, noticing now that Brooke has been looking at me, not at Andrew.

She walks over to me now, and her arms envelope me in a hug. *How does she always know exactly what to do?*

I continue to hug her, trying to match my breathing to hers as I look at my brother. I have to remind myself that Andrew is alive. The doctors believe that when he heals, he will be okay. I need to focus on that.

Looking at his leg, though, I'm reminded of why he is injured in the first place, and the guilt and pain of that memory floods me with anxiety.

A sick feeling fills my stomach, and I know that no matter how much I want to be with Andrew, I can't be around him right now if I am going to stay sane.

"I need to leave. Not for the whole time but I can't look at him right now." My voice cracks into Brooke's hair. She nods against me, and as she pulls away, she looks into my eyes.

"It's okay to leave. We can come back another time."

I still don't know how she's taking this so well, but I'm grateful for it no matter the reason.

"I was thinking about just walking for a little bit," I say. "My mom told me there's a garden on the fifth floor. Do you want to stay here or walk with me?"

"I'll come with you," she says, but turning to my mom, she adds, "unless you would like me to stay with you, Ms. Carter?" I see the kind smile on my mom's face when she responds, but it is one with pain under the surface, nonetheless.

"That's alright, Brooke. You two go walk for a little while. I'll text you when I'm ready to go, or if you want to come back in, you know where to go." Then she looks back to my brother.

We walk into the hallway, heading toward the elevators and making the short ride down to the fifth floor where there is indeed a garden.

I hold the door open for Brooke as she walks out into the garden, breathing out the word, "Wow." I follow her gaze, looking at the outdoor garden.

It is quite beautiful. Flowers have been planted in rows, but there are also vines of ivy wrapped around iron gates to make arches, succulents, and a water fountain. Next to the fountain is a bench, and as we look around the garden a bit more, we head toward it.

When we sit, we don't speak for a while. I know that there is so much to say, and at the same time, I don't know how to say it. Brooke leans against me and I place an arm around her, hugging her to me to have something, anything, grounding me. I'm not sure how long it is before Brooke finally speaks first.

"I know that was hard. It was hard for me, and Andrew wasn't even too close of a friend of mine. I don't have the right words to say, not that I'm sure there are any, so I'm just going to say I'm sorry."

I shake my head, slightly laughing. "You have nothing to be sorry for."

"I don't mean it like that. I mean I'm sorry you have to be in this position, you, alive and discharged with your brother in the state he is in."

"It really isn't fair, any of it."

"No, it isn't."

We're silent for another chunk of time. The fountain and the occasional bird sounds are the only noises we hear, and as I turn my focus toward these two sounds, I feel my eyelids close and give in to sleep.

My eyes flutter open to something shaking me. After I blink a few times, I see that Brooke is rattling my arm, and when I try to focus on what she's saying, my mind starts to clear.

"Jackson, wake up."

I know she wouldn't be waking me up this forcefully if something wasn't wrong, and I jolt awake.

"What's wrong? Is Andrew okay?" I search her face for concern, but she only looks happy.

"He's fine, Jackson. He's fine, and he is awake. The doctors decided that he was ready an hour or so ago. Your mom just called and said he is asking for you." Her words hit me like a ton of bricks, yet every part of me feels electrified.

He's okay. He's awake.

"Can we see him?" I ask her.

"Yes, I figured you'd want to go see him right away, so I told your mom we were on the way up."

"Then let's go!"

We take the elevator to the fifteenth floor. Before I even reach the door to Andrew's room, I can see nurses and doctors rushing in, which should be expected considering he just woke up from a coma.

I take a deep breath, reaching my hand out to Brooke's to steady myself. She squeezes me gently. I'm ready.

Walking into the room, I see there isn't a lot of space, not that there was before because of all the doctors and nurses. Several of them are checking Andrew's reflexes, his pupils, looking at his leg, and as I watch them, I realize he is still slightly disoriented.

I almost figured Andrew wouldn't notice me due to all the distractions.

I was wrong.

The moment I step closer to the bed, his eyes lock with mine and a smile reaches his eyes. Brooke is standing beside me, still holding my hand, and his eyes flick between us.

"Look at my welcome people."

Andrew always was one for jokes at a serious time, but I recognize his slowness in speaking, and I wonder if this is normal for a coma patient or if it's a bad sign. Thankfully, his doctors answer my silent question.

"Don't worry. This is perfectly normal for a patient just waking up." I sigh in relief, as does my mom.

Brooke leans against my shoulder, and the world stops. At

this moment, it's just the three of us. We are all happy, and I don't want to waste a second of it.

After Andrew gets situated, his doctors check him out, and he has about a million labs ordered before we finally get to spend some time with him.

Because of his coma, it takes him a while to speak proficiently, recall memories, and he is slow to respond to most anything. Yet, no matter how much effort it takes, he wants to talk to us, hear from us about what he has missed, and just be with us.

We stay in his room, Brooke sitting on the edge of his bed, me behind her, and my mom in the reclining chair until a nurse has to come in to let us know that visiting hours are over.

I try to convince my mom to stay with him and let me handle the girls, but she is adamant that she has to take them somewhere in the morning and that I need my own rest.

When we leave, I give my brother a huge hug, trying not to hurt him, but he hugs me back with a force I remember. He's regained some strength already.

Walking to the car, I feel the tension leave my body knowing Andrew is okay. I turn to Brooke before we reach the car to give her a hug.

She laughs as I do, asking me, "What was that for?" when I pull away.

"I'm happy. I thought it would be a lot harder to be happy after everything, but I am." I sigh, but mostly to let go of tension.

She then pulls me into a hug of her own. It's a faster one than mine since my mom is waiting for us to get into the car.

When she leans back, I reach to the side and open her door. She climbs in and I follow, shutting both of our doors behind us.

My brother is awake. Brooke is here, and she isn't leaving me. We're alive. Maybe, just maybe, we'll be okay. Maybe we can survive this.

Chapter 6
Before

We can't survive this if we are here for much longer. There isn't enough food for all six of us, and if I don't find some today, we're going to have to start rationing what little food we already have. After I got up this morning, I tried as a last effort to see if any of our phones were working. Most were shattered, and the others were dead. Luckily, however, the wind from yesterday is gone, as is the falling snow, so the temperature must be higher today.

It's definitely later in the afternoon—probably closer to one or two—even though nobody else is awake. We all had quite a traumatic day yesterday, though, so we deserve a few more hours of sleep. But I know that soon enough people will wake up, and they will be hungry for food we don't have.

I remember the car that hit us is down here too, and I wonder if they have any supplies that could help us, or maybe even a working phone. I know that it's an endeavor none of us want to take, but we can't live down here. Especially if we don't know how long it will be.

As I'm thinking about this, Andrew stirs awake without waking the little girl. He looks at me, and I gesture for him to meet me outside. He nods and opens the door. I do the same, walking to meet him at his door.

"They're all going to wake up hungry," I say quietly, so as not to wake the child still sleeping on him. "Not just today, but however many days we're going to be stuck down here. The other car might have some food we can eat. You know we didn't pack much food at all. And they might have a phone that is working. It's not likely, but it is worth a shot." My last words come out in a shiver as the cold crawls down my neck.

He nods, thinking about what I said. I know he wants to go. Of course, he does—he wouldn't be who he is if he didn't. But he also knows that the little girl is clinging to him. I can tell he doesn't want to leave her.

"I can go," I say, but before I can even get the next words out, he cuts me off.

"No. I'm going."

"Why don't we both go? The car isn't that far away," I say.

"Because she," he says, gesturing to the little girl, "cannot wake up without someone also being awake. She already did that yesterday and the others were dead. I'm not doing that to her again."

I understand, and I know he isn't going to let me go. He must do something, and simply caring for her isn't enough, even with his injured leg.

"Give her to me. Carefully," I say. We carefully transfer her to my arms.

"Thank you," he says when she is in my arms. I watch as he limps toward the car. I look up in the sky and see that the sun is a little angled above me, confirming my original thought that it was early in the afternoon.

I walk back to where I was in the car, slowly and carefully, sitting back into my seat after gently opening the door. I look over at Brooke, seeing that she is waking up.

"Hi," she whispers, looking over at me. "Thank you for letting me use your flannel last night." I shake my head, knowing that this "thank you" battle isn't going to end anytime soon.

"Of course. You can use it for however long we're here," I say. It was cold last night, even with the towels blocking the snow, but that backpack was not going to be comfortable, and the flannel probably wouldn't have done me that much good anyway.

"Where's Andrew?" she asks me. I shake my head and explain the conversation I had a few moments ago and why I was now holding this little girl.

"You're right, you know," she says. "If we're stuck here much longer, we won't be in a good place. I'd be lying if I didn't say I was worried."

I know she's right. That's why it was the first thing on my mind this morning. There was plenty of snow on the ground from earlier in the week when we got here, even though it hasn't been actively snowing too heavily where we are camped. That's why when I see Andrew hobbling back a few minutes later with a small cooler and a few other supplies in his other hand, as well as a jacket and what looks like a blanket over his shoulder. Relief flushes through me. Brooke and I climb out of the car, waking Lydia in the process, and walk over to where he is standing.

"What's going on?" Lydia asks. Then she sees the little girl in my arms. A curious look passes on her face then.

"We'll fill you in. Just a second," Brooke says.

Almost as if the little girl senses that Andrew has returned, she wakes up with sleepy eyes. I see a slight fear in them when she sees me, but upon seeing Andrew, it disappears. He sets down what he brought back and walks over to me, taking her in his arms. I walk over to where he put down the jacket after he jerks his head to it to suggest I try it on and put my arms through the sleeves. It's a slightly tight fit, but it works. Then I look at the blanket, which is thick and fluffy. Perfect for night.

A part of me feels sick wearing a dead person's clothes. A huge part of me. But another part of me, a scared part, is grateful because last night was cold, even with the fire. Then I hear Andrew talking to the girl.

"Hi, I'm Andrew. What's your name?" he asks her in the same gentle voice he uses with our younger sisters.

"Emily," she says quietly with more of a W on the latter part of her name.

"Nice to meet you, Emily. How old are you?"

She responds with an even quieter, "Five", which means I was way off on my estimate.

"Well, Emily, this is Lydia, Brooke, and Jackson. Lucas is in the car," he says, pointing at each of us when he says our names.

"Where is Mommy and Daddy? Where is Matty?" she asks Andrew, so quietly I almost don't hear her. So, I was right, as I had feared. It was her family in the car.

"They can't be here right now. Have they ever told you about a place where all the angels are?" he asks her, and she nods. "What did they tell you about it?"

"Everyone is happy, and Grandma and Grandpa are up there with all the animals," she says, making my heart hurt at her innocence.

"Yeah, that is exactly right. That is where Mommy, Daddy, and Matty are. They're playing with all the animals and with Grandma and Grandpa, and they're happy."

She looks at him, almost as though she is questioning him, but then she nods. Then Andrew turns to look at me.

"The cooler has very little food—it looks like they were returning from a trip, or something, based on how much was left over. No working phones, though. There's also her backpack, a pair of binoculars, a single tent with some poles and something else I can show you later." He says the last part pointedly, meaning he didn't want to say it with Emily around.

"What food did they have?" Brooke asks, sounding hopeful.

"There were a lot of cracked eggs in the other cooler with tiny scraps of leftover meat that some animals got to. Everything else I could find is in that cooler. There were two or so candy bars, a box of half-eaten nuts, and a couple water bottles." I can see Brooke doing the math in her head, but she and I know that could last us only a few days max.

"Well," she says in a voice that I know is meant to make the others feel hopeful, "I think we should have a little something to eat to celebrate." She picks up the cooler and moves to where the fire was burning last night, which is now covered in snow.

She takes out one candy bar and splits it into six pieces, handing one to each of us except Lucas, but Andrew shakes his head, telling her to give his piece to Emily. At first, Brooke insists, but he doesn't relent, so she ends up giving it to Emily. We all eat the candy like it's our lifeline, and once it's gone, we all want more.

Brooke then pulls Lydia aside, and I can see the moment that Lydia completely understands what happens. Her already pale complexion turns paler, and she looks beyond Brooke in the direction of the car and back at Emily. There is worry in her eyes.

After reassuring Lydia, Brooke goes over to the car to wake Lucas for breakfast. I sit down on a log near the car, trying to figure out what we're going to do. Now we have a tent, but that isn't going to protect us from the cold winter. Even worse—and I didn't want to bring this up to Brooke or anyone else, for that matter—I know that this time of year combined with where we are in Colorado is the worst combination weather-wise for us to be stuck down here. Our only saving grace is that there isn't a snowstorm yet. Still, we only have a few days before we will get hypothermia. If we keep our clothes from getting too wet, and we get rescued sometime soon, we won't start to lose feeling in our limbs.

Soon, we're going to be stuck in slightly colder weather, and none of us have the right clothing or protection from anything much colder to be even close to not worrying about our safety. We have to get out of here. *I* have to get everyone out of here.

Then Brooke walks up to me, a look on her face I know can't be anything good. She sits down on the log with me and leans over to whisper into my ear, "Lucas isn't waking up. I'm worried he is starting to get hypothermic, if he isn't already. He's breathing, but I think he was running on adrenaline yesterday. His head injury was bad, probably worse than I could even have said, and I was shocked he was even awake. But this means he has something wrong which I can't treat, out here or otherwise. He needs medical attention, and he needs it fast."

She leans back to look at me meaningfully, letting me know she is serious. This is bad.

"Is he stable for now?" I ask her, wanting to be sure before we make any decisions.

"For now."

I look over at my brother, catching his eyes and letting him know, silently, that Brooke has to talk to him. He acknowledges my look and walks over to me with Emily. I also look at Lydia, making sure she gets the message and walks over to me.

"Hey, Emily," I say. "Can we go try to play something?" She nods eagerly at me, making me happy she is getting more comfortable with us. "Okay then, let's go try to find a good throwing rock and see who throws it the farthest."

I take her hand and walk toward the clearing behind a few trees that are near our campsite, stopping to pick up the binoculars quickly. Looking back, I can see the worried look on both Lydia and Andrew's faces, and I know they are getting to realize how bad our situation is now. Again, I look up the mountain, trying to see the road even a little bit, but there is no luck. The climb would be impossibly dangerous, and the chill air combined with the snow block any visibility we might have had.

The clearing is a little different than I thought it would be. I guess where we landed is a plateau on the mountainside, and out beyond the clearing is another drop, this one maybe fifty or sixty feet. It almost looks like there is a hiking path down to the bottom of the cliff Emily and I stand on, and when I look closer, I see it isn't a frequently traveled path, but a path nonetheless. For the first time in two days, I feel a little hope.

At the bottom of the cliff is a wooded terrain, slightly sparce from all the dying trees. Where the plateau sits, we are a little below the tree line, so we are looking between the sparce trees, but I can see far enough out that I feel a little anxiety over our situation start to creep into my mind. I try to shove it aside and return to Emily.

"Okay. We need to look for one rock each. It needs to be flat and smooth, got it?" She bobs her head up and down. "Okay, go find one." She goes hunting for the perfect rock, and I look around before landing on a flat one that seems perfect for skipping if we were on a lake. I pick mine up, and Emily runs back over with hers.

I bring the binoculars up to my eyes and see a tree I want her to aim for. It is a little taller than the others around it, so I know she'll be able to spot it "Alright, you go first. You see that tree down there, the one that's a little taller than the rest," I say, handing her the binoculars and pointing them to the tree. She does so eagerly, and when she meets my eyes, I know she has seen it. "Okay, you have to hit that one to win, okay?" Convinced it isn't too far to hit, she smirks, and I smile at how innocent she is.

"Go for it," I say, and she winds her arm far back and swings it forward as hard as she can. The rock flies from her hand and lands far, considering how small she is.

"Woah!" I emphasize for her. "You almost hit that tree! And here I was thinking that there was no way anyone could hit it!"

She laughs at me, clearly proud of herself.

"Well, there is no way I can hit it, but I have to try." She puts the binoculars up to her eyes to watch as I throw the rock, and I purposefully aim at the tree but throw it in the wrong direction. She starts laughing hysterically over the fact that I threw it in the wrong direction.

"You didn't throw it at the tree! You threw it at the car." Her words shock me for a moment. What car? What could she mean?

"What car, Emily?" I say, spinning around and looking.

"That one," she says, pointing in the distance, still looking through the binoculars. I follow her hand, taking the binoculars from her and looking to where she is pointing. I see that only a few miles in the distance, is a car, *next to a cabin*. It is between the trees on top of a hill, so it would be slightly obscured if you didn't look closely, which is why I didn't immediately notice it. My rock couldn't have nearly come close to hitting it, but it must have passed in front of her line of sight for her to see the car. Somebody's car. Somebody's cabin. *Rescue.*

What if ideas run rampant. What if there is food? Supplies?

A phone? A radio? Help of any kind? I know it would be stupid to try to get there—it is in the distance through some likely dangerous forestry with animals, and we may get lost—but would be even more stupid not to go.

Which is why I tell Emily that she won and that we should probably head back. She is disappointed we don't get to keep playing, but she walks back happily when I tell her we'll do it again some other time. The second we get back, she runs to Andrew to tell him how she won, and I pull Brooke aside.

"There's a cabin," I say, hope in my voice. "When we were throwing rocks, Emily said that I was aiming at a car, and when I looked, I saw a car and a cabin. They're both a bit far, and it might be risky, but it's risky staying here too."

She wears a shocked expression that transitions to a pensive one before she responds. "I agree that it's not the ideal option, but we aren't going to make it here for much longer. We need to go, but we have to be smart about how we do it. We can't just charge into the wild unprepared—it's too dangerous." She is right, of course, but I am so grateful she agrees that it is worth trying.

But it is dangerous telling Andrew since he would want to charge off right now. Yet, he's my twin, and even if he wasn't, he's also stuck in this. So, it wouldn't be fair to not tell him. Brooke and I agree to let the group know.

Lydia is already sitting with Andrew and Emily, so Brooke takes Lydia aside for a minute to explain what is happening, and that she wants her to take Emily so we can talk to Andrew. Lydia pulls Emily aside, and Andrew looks between Brooke and I questioningly.

"There is a cabin," I say, and immediately I see the look in his eyes that I feared. "It's a bit far in the distance, and it wouldn't be smart to just charge out there right now, especially because it looks like a four mile walk just to get there."

"We have to go," he says, looking at me as though I'm crazy for even suggesting we wait.

"That's the problem. We can't just go. Emily would never be able to walk that far, especially in this cold. Lucas is incapacitated right now, and we can't just carry him. And even if those weren't problems, the trees could be the way. We don't know what is out there. There might be nothing, and that is highly unlikely. There might be everything."

I know what I'm saying is true, yet I want to leave just as badly. Brooke's rationality is what is keeping me from running out there right now.

"We can go out there when we have a better idea of what we can handle," Brooke says. "You certainly couldn't walk that far. Your leg may be able to handle carrying a cooler one hundred feet, but that is a far distance." Part of me wishes Brooke hadn't added that last part because my twin is not only stubborn, but he loves a challenge. However, he isn't going to make his decisions based on what she tells him.

I see the stubbornness in his eyes, and I expect him to fight me on this for a while longer, but instead he says, "Okay. You're right. We'll go tomorrow though."

Brooke and I exchange looks, and our eyes agree with him.

"Tomorrow, I promise. For the rest of the day, we rest. There aren't that many hours left in this day anyway," I say pointing at the darkening sky above me. Andrew's eyes say something he isn't, however. Then he reaches behind him.

"The thing I didn't want to say earlier—it was this knife," he says, producing what looks like a hunting knife in a leather sheath of sorts. "I have a feeling you could use it, boy scout."

"Thanks. I probably can, for the fire tonight."

He gives me a thumbs up, getting up to go find Lydia and Emily.

Brooke turns to me, saying, "That was easier than I thought it would be, considering."

"Maybe he realized how injured he is, or maybe he understood it's too dangerous. Either way, I'm happy he's waiting until tomorrow. Knowing him, he'd charge into that wooded area without so much as a pair of shoes on if he had to."

Brooke laughs, and I join her.

It feels good to laugh. After what feels like forever not laughing, feeling scared and worried about what comes next, it feels like tension is being erased in my shoulders, my legs, my lungs just a little. I smile at Brooke, and she does the same. It feels good to do that again. For a moment, I feel certain we'll be okay.

And as the sky darkens, I gather more materials for another fire, again clearing the area where the fire was last night. This time, however, I have a tent I can use. I take the knife that Andrew gave me and cut the floor of the tent out, as well as the cover to the front. I take the floor, cutting it into a few pieces, and replace the towels with them to make the car a little warmer at night.

I then take the rest of the tent and use it to cover where I'm putting the fire. There is plenty of space around the flames, so they won't burn the tent itself. Hopefully, this time, the snow won't be able to get to it. I use the lighter to start the fire in the brush I collected and place it in the center. The heat drifts forward toward the opening of the tent, and I think that the heat might travel into the car enough to keep us just that much warmer. It seems to do just that after a little while, so I join the others for our "dinner."

We all eat another piece of candy bar, Andrew again giving up his piece for Emily, and Brooke does this as well this time. She said she wasn't hungry, but I know that is a lie, so I give her mine.

"I'm actually not hungry. You're just too nice to say you are," I say to her. She smiles at me, but instead of rejecting it like I thought she would, she takes it gratefully.

When we all finish eating, I can see we're all exhausted. Even though we haven't done much, the weather is starting to wear on all of us. None of us want to admit it, but it's true.

We all walk over to the car, climbing inside. I distribute the blankets, both Lydia and Brooke being extremely thankful and Emily hugging me. Lydia and Brooke, seeing this, laugh and give me a hug, too. I laugh with them, but the hugs warm my heart.

Then Emily asks me if she could sleep with me tonight, to which I say, "Of course." She bundles up on top of me, hugging me like she did Andrew the other night. I look over at Brooke, who is smiling against my flannel made into a pillow. She silently mouths, "Thank you," and I do the same.

And then we go to sleep, this time a little warmer and feeling just a little more hopeful.

Chapter 7
After

The drive back home is rough, especially because it's dark. The hospital is a high rise of lights behind us, and as we drive away, I stare ahead, out of the front windshield, into the darkness ahead of us.

I know my mom is a good driver, but the fog is picking up around us and people's lights are hard to see, increasing my anxiety. On top of that, my mom is driving much quicker than one should in the fog.

Oddly enough, Brooke is sitting next to me now, even though she was sitting in the front seat when we left. *Maybe I fell asleep,* I wonder to myself.

A car honks behind us, telling us to move faster, and when I look back, I see a snow-covered road behind us. I feel the car move faster as my mom increases her weight on the gas pedal, and I almost tell her to slow down.

I glance over at Brooke. The clear blue eyes I normally can't get enough of are looking painfully into my own, terrified, and that is when I decide to speak up.

"Mom, please slow down. You're scaring Brooke and me," I plead with her, but she doesn't respond. My heart races faster, and when I look ahead of us, my pulse thunders harder and harder.

Because a car is coming right at us. It's happening again. Time feels like it's moving so slowly, and yet I can anticipate exactly what's going to happen as the headlights get closer and closer to us.

Then my eyes fly open as I hear Brooke yelling my name, not too loud, but loud enough to draw my attention to her voice. Suddenly, the realization hits me: it was a dream. Or more accurately, a nightmare.

Brooke is standing next to my bed where I am lying, panting with my heart still racing. She has her hands on my bare shoulders from where she was shaking me to wake me up. Her eyes are wide, almost as wide as they seemed in my nightmare, but they're not filled with fear, just concern.

"Are you okay?" she asks me as I sit up against the headboard. I nod slowly, focusing on my surroundings and leaning over to turn on the lamp on my bedside table.

"Yeah. I guess I was having a nightmare." I motion for her to sit down on my bed, and she does, sitting cross-legged in front of me.

"You were yelling. I thought maybe you were hurt. I'm surprised your mom didn't hear you."

"She's always been an extremely light sleeper, so she

sleeps with one of those headbands that block sounds," I say to Brooke. She nods, and we're silent for a little longer. I am suddenly very aware of my bare chest and look around my room for a sweatshirt or T-shirt to cover up with. Thankfully, on the side of my bed there is a grey Target sweatshirt which I lean down and grab before pulling it over my head. When I glance back at Brooke's eyes staring at me, she blushes and looks away. *What was that about?*

"Do you want to talk about it?" she then asks me, rubbing her eyes with the edge of her long-sleeved shirt before finally looking back at me.

"I don't know," I say, slightly embarrassed.

"Come on," she says, pushing me playfully, so I relent.

"Alright, well we were driving back here from the hospital, and it was dark. My mom was driving really fast, and I wanted her to slow down. Then there was a car behind us that was honking to make us drive faster." I sigh, remembering how I felt at this point in the dream.

"My mom sped the car up, you and I were very concerned, fearful even. Then I saw headlights in the front windshield, and right before the car hit us you woke me up," I explain, and Brooke looks at me, her lip pulled between her teeth. *That is so distracting.*

"Are you okay now?" she asks me, and I give her a reassuring tired grin.

We're silent for a second, and then she speaks looking down at her hands. "Did you see that the school sent an email out to everyone?"

I give her a confused look, and she puts her hand out for

me to hand her my phone. I give it to her, and she pulls up my email, showing me the unopened message.

Dear Mr. Carter,

As I am sure you are aware, five of our current undergraduate students were involved in an auto vehicle accident on US 550, resulting in their car having gone over the mountainside. All five of our students survived, but two remain in critical conditions. The parents of each of the following students or the students themselves have allowed us to use the student's names.

Andrew Carter is currently in the ICU at Chesterton Hospital in Colorado, but I have been informed he is recovering from his coma currently and is gaining his strength back.

His brother, Jackson Carter, has been released alongside Brooke Hastings and Lydia Drake, from Johnson Hospital in Colorado.

Lucas Montgomery remains in critical condition, currently in the ICU at Chesterton Hospital in Colorado. His family has been with him, and we look forward to his recovery.

Our hearts go out to the survivors of this terrible accident. Please keep each of the members of this tragedy in your thoughts and prayers.

I suck in a deep breath after reading the letter. It was an automated message sent to each student. I know that our names were on every new station in the Colorado area, so it isn't hard for me to imagine that everyone already knew what was going on. Still, the fact that everyone knows about our accident makes me feel nervous. I do remember my mom asking me if it was okay if my coach was kept in the loop and updated the school while I was in the hospital, so I guess it doesn't surprise me how much he knew about our accident.

"What did you think?" Brooke asks me, and I shrug.

"I think that it feels like I'm reading about some news story, but it was really about us. It's so factual, and yet feels so personal. I don't know how to feel."

"I get that. It does feel weird. I feel like we haven't even had the chance to recover completely, and the world won't let us." She sighs deeply before continuing. "I've been thinking about returning to school and all of that. It's hard to imagine that something like this can happen and people expect you to get over it quickly." She looks at the wall, turning her head away from me slightly. "I don't know. I feel shaken by it all, and yet I don't want to miss out on living because of it, you know?" She turns back to look at me, waiting for me to answer her question.

"Yeah. I get it," I say. "I want to take it day by day, but I know I have to jump back in. I'm sure that Coach is going to ask when I'm coming back soon. I had a competition right after Christmas that I was going to do, but now I'm not so sure."

The truth is I hadn't wanted to think about it. I have been more jittery thinking about getting back out there and snowboarding after everything. Still, I don't want to disappoint anyone, and not going back would mean exactly that.

"What do you mean you're not so sure? You love snowboarding, or at least you loved it. Anyone who watched you compete could see that you and the board have a connection," Brooke says, and she is voicing exactly what I fear others might say.

"I don't know. Part of me thinks about how the accident woke me up to living life for more than just snowboarding.

Part of me also wonders if I get back on the board, will I be the same?" I sigh, not sure if she understands me, but she nods, urging me to continue.

"It's just that I don't want to be living for anyone's expectations, and I realize that any day now I'm going to get an email from Coach asking me when I'm coming back. I don't know what I'm going to say. I haven't even been on a board since Thanksgiving. I was going to practice over break, but I don't even know how I feel about it now."

I see in her eyes that she understands what I'm telling her. It's funny, I think, that it's easier to talk to Brooke than it ever has been to anyone else.

Even talking to Andrew sometimes feels like he doesn't completely get me. Sometimes, I guess, I don't need the person who is the replica of me to tell me what I already know.

"Okay, well that is going to be on our to-do list," Brooke says. "We're going to get you on a board before Christmas, and you can decide for yourself what your future holds, not your coach, not your mom, not me—you." She says this so confidently that I grin at her, shaking my head, but not out of disagreement.

Then her face turns down a little bit, like something is bothering her. "Have you thought at all about Emily?" Her voice is quiet, quieter than it has been.

When we were first at the hospital, I asked about her, but her doctors would tell me anything for a while. I had finally got Jake to find out if she could have visitors or not, and when I heard she could, I went to her room. She was non-compliant with her nurses and doctors to the point where they had to restrain her. I talked with her, trying to get her to understand that the doctors and nurses were there to help her, and I think she started to understand.

Her case worker finally came in, so I tried to leave to give them privacy, but Emily wouldn't let me leave. I had to listen to the case worker explain how none of her family members wanted to take her in since she was a part of a trauma that they assumed makes her damaged. When the case worker was leaving, I got her information, and gave her mine and my mom's in case she needed anything and so that Emily could keep in contact with me if she wanted to.

After I left that day, Emily got discharged to a foster family, and I haven't heard anything from her since. I despise the fact that Emily now has to uproot her entire life because of her own family. Brooke and I had talked about this while we were in the hospital, and she was torn to have heard how her family was treating her. We both felt that her situation was heart wrenching for anyone, but especially a five-year old.

"I have. I just keep thinking that it is unfair, what happened to her," I say, sighing.

"She is such a little kid, and none of her family wants her. She doesn't deserve anything that has happened in the past few weeks," Brooke says.

I shake my head too and feel my heart ache a little bit. "I plan to reach out to her case worker and meet with her at some point. I just want to be in her life, and after everything, she deserves to be with someone who cares about her."

"I agree with you, and I'd love to come, too, if that is alright?" she asks.

"Of course," I say, surprised that she would think I would say no. We just sit in the quiet of the house, then. The only noise I can hear is the fan whirring around us, and Brooke stares up at it as it spins around.

I look over at my bedside table, glancing at the clock, and see that it's still only three a.m. I don't feel tired anymore, now fully awake from being startled, and wonder whether I should try to sleep or not.

Brooke shifts again, and I wonder if she is no longer feeling comfortable being in here. I don't exactly know how to ask her, so instead I think of something to do.

"Well, I don't think I'm going to fall back asleep anytime soon, so do you want to watch a movie or something?" I ask her, and she looks up at me, grinning in affirmation.

I pat the area on the left side of my bed that has not been slept in, and under the comforter while I get up to grab my laptop from the desk where it was charging.

When I get back into my bed, I open Netflix, the main page appearing on my screen. I then wonder what exactly Brooke wants to watch, but before I know it, she is scrolling along the touchpad and selecting Knight and Day, an action and comedy movie.

I smile at her selection, having watched the movie myself already, but honestly, I would be willing to watch anything that she wants to watch. I just like being with her.

She clicks play after looking up at me to make sure I'm alright with her choice, and when she does, she gets a bit more comfortable in my bed. I do the same, trying to angle the screen so I'm comfortable and can see fine.

The movie can't be more than thirty minutes in when I feel my eyes drooping. I've been looking next to me periodically throughout the movie at Brooke to make sure she is still awake, but when I look now, she's fast asleep.

When I blink, my eyes feel heavy, and while in the background I hear the movie playing, I can't necessarily understand it. I think I move my hands to close the laptop, but whether I am successful or not I don't know.

All I know is that I feel the heaviness on my eyelids weigh heavier and heavier, and finally I give in, allowing myself to relax.

I wake up when I hear the taunting voice of my sister saying, "Ooh, Brooke and Jackson are sleeping together!" I rub my face, looking to my left and seeing that Brooke is indeed still sleeping but stirring slightly.

"Kayla, we *were* sleeping. You woke me up," I add, knowing that no matter what I say, she's going to continue taunting us.

"Well Mom wanted me to wake you up so that you can eat breakfast before we leave." She then runs out of my room quickly, still saying over and over, "Brooke and Jackson are sleeping together." I'm sure my mom is going to love that.

Beside me, Brooke is finally awake, and when she looks around her and doesn't recognize where she is, I notice she is startled. Then, when she sees me and the open laptop in the center of the bed, she asks what time it is.

I look over at the side table to look for the time, and when I read that it says seven fifteen, I relay the information to her.

"Did I hear something about breakfast?"

"Yeah. I have a feeling my mom made pancakes since that is her specialty when we have people over." Her mouth turns upward at the edges, and the sunlight through my windows illuminates her blue irises. *How can her eyes be so captivating?*

We both get out of my bed, Brooke pulls the comforter up to the edge of the bed so that it looks neater, and then we head out my door to go downstairs for food.

When we reach the bottom of the stairs, the familiar smell of my mom's amazing pancakes surrounds me. My brother and I used to beg my mom to make these all the time when we were kids, and even this past Thanksgiving when I was over, I begged her to make them. I don't know why they're so special, since she won't tell us how she makes them, but I love them anyway.

We sit down at the island as my mom pours the batter into the pan, dancing around the kitchen with an apron on. My sisters' plates are already in the sink, and she has three other plates laid out in front of her.

She is playing some music at a very loud volume and dancing to the beat of it, making me chuckle. She did this a lot when the girls were born, and she was trying to stop them from crying.

I remember this one day where our mom was cleaning our yard, and while my sisters were playing, Kayla hit her head. She started to bawl, and no matter what Andrew or I did, she wouldn't stop. Finally, I went and got my mom, and when she came into the house she immediately started to play 'I Wanna Dance With Somebody' by Whitney Houston on full volume.

She started to jump around, singing at the top of her lungs, and we couldn't help but laugh. Kayla stopped crying and started to jump with my mom, and soon enough we all joined in. From then on out, it was an unspoken rule that if we were playing music and dancing, no one could be upset. Watching my mom now, I can feel that same happiness.

Finally, our pancakes are ready, and as soon as they're placed in front of us, Brooke says, "I hear these are your specialty. Tell me how to make them perfect."

My mom smiles at her and spreads a little butter on each pancake, followed by some berries and opens her hands as if to say *voila*.

My mom and I watch as Brooke takes her first bite, and a contented look passes on her face as she chews, placing two thumbs up in front of her.

My mom cheers, clapping her hands, and then goes to do the same to her own pancakes, eating behind the island as she stands.

We eat all our pancakes, music blasting in the background, and when we finish, I maneuver around the counter to help my mom.

"I know you need to take the girls somewhere. Let me clean-up for you," I say.

"Me too," Brooke pipes up. "The pancakes were amazing, Ms. Carter." She says this enthusiastically, but my mom waves a hand in front of her face.

"Thank you both, it would be a big help. And Brooke? You don't need to call me Ms. Carter, honey. Beverly is perfectly fine."

Brooke nods, a grin returning to her face, and internally, I thank my mom for bringing that back.

My mom leaves the kitchen, calling for my sisters, and I say to Brooke, "Do you want to wash or dry? We don't have a dishwasher here."

"I'll wash," she says. I move to the side so that she can wash the five plates and utensils, and I grab a dish towel to dry.

We move quickly enough, and when I finish placing the last dish in the cabinet, Brooke turns to me and asks, "So what are we doing today?"

As soon as she says this, however, the landline rings loudly, and because I know my mom has enough to do, I yell, "I've got it." I place one finger in front of me to say one minute to Brooke and go grab the phone.

It rings four times before I can pick it up, and when I do, I say, "Carter residence. This is Jackson. May I ask who's calling?" There's no response for a moment, and I almost repeat myself, but then the caller responds.

"This is Jackson Carter?" the female voice asks.

"Yes, who am I speaking to?"

"My name is Kamri Hastings. I'm Brooke Hastings's sister. I was wondering if I could speak with her?"

Now it's my turn to freeze and not respond.

Brooke looks at me, confused, as I probably have quite an odd look on my face. I don't know how exactly to tell her that her sister is calling.

"It's um," I say, covering the speaker part of the phone, "Kamri."

Her face freezes into a look that I am sure mimics my own.

How do you respond to your sister who you haven't spoken to in almost two years?

"She wants to talk to you," I add, and Brooke pauses for a moment before extending her hand, the shock still clear on her face.

She cautiously takes the phone and places it against her ear hesitantly before saying, "Hello?" in a shaky voice.

Kamri must have said something, because the tears start to form in Brooke's eyes. Her hands are shaking so much that she can't hold the phone against her ear as easily, so she pulls it away from her ear and presses the speakerphone button.

"—and I'm going to be in Montrose tomorrow, so I wanted to know if you wanted to meet up somewhere for coffee or lunch or really anything?" Kamri finishes asking Brooke her question, and Brooke is still stunned so much that she cannot respond without choking on her words, even though she is nodding.

I walk over to Brooke, hugging her while I say to Kamri, "Hey this is Jackson again. You're on speakerphone. I think Brooke would love to meet up with you tomorrow. Do you have somewhere specific in mind?"

Kamri responds quickly, saying, "Oh great! When I visited near Montrose, I loved this little brunch place called Tin Box. It has a bit of everything."

Brooke finally turns toward the phone and says in a shaky voice, "Would it be alright if Jackson joined us?"

"Of course, he can come," she says. "I'll make the reservation for ten-thirty tomorrow, if that's alright?"

Brooke nods against me again, and I can tell she can't

speak more right now.

"Yeah, Kamri. That sounds great. We'll be there tomorrow." I say this in a cheery voice, even though I'm not sure exactly how Brooke feels about the lunch date. She seems like she wants to go, but I can't completely tell.

"Alright, great. See you tomorrow then!" she says before hanging up. The phone sits in Brooke's hand, playing the dial tone over and over. Finally, I take the phone and press the end-call button. The dial tone turns off and we stand in silence.

Brooke hugs me tighter. I can't explain exactly why but I feel that in that moment that is my exact purpose, to be there, to hug her, to make her feel like she is okay.

A little while later, Brooke and I decide to get cleaned up a little so we each go shower, she in the guest room and I in my own bathroom. I told her that when she was finished, we could head to the small Target by my house and get a movie and some snacks, and her eyes had lit up. *I love when they light up.*

I finished showering before her and threw on some jeans with a white T-shirt and a flannel that looked very similar to the flannel I gave to Brooke. She had insisted after the crash that the hospital let my mom take the flannel home to clean so she could keep it, and they let her. So, when Brooke walked downstairs to meet me wearing it, I grinned at her.

"Are you trying to match me?" I ask her, and she laughs back at me.

"No, I just like this flannel," she says, beaming with a grin. When she reaches me, I pull her in for a hug and I realize that while it's only slight, her hair still smells florally. It's odd because the soap in the guest shower doesn't smell like that, so I ask her.

"Oh, it's a shampoo that I normally use. I asked your mom to pick it up once they released me and told her I would pay her back, but she wouldn't let me. It has a rose and vanilla scent. Do you like it?" she asks, an innocent look in her eyes. Do I like it? *It smells like her, so of course I do.*

"I really do. I noticed it when we were in the car that first day, and again right now. It smells really good." She blushes slightly before tugging my arm toward the door.

"I was promised a movie and snacks," she says in a sing-song voice. I have no choice but to follow her. How could I not?

We make the short walk to Target and once inside pick up some popcorn, Reese's Pieces—which Brooke claims are the best candy in the world, possibly tied with Sour Patch Watermelon, which we couldn't find—and some Mug Root Beer. I ask her why so specific, and she says that we need top-tier snacks and drinks for a top-tier movie. Then we walk to the movie aisle, and she immediately gets stuck on The Princess Bride, which I had seen once or twice but she insists that we have to get it. I grab it from the aisle before walking to the register where I see a small bag of Sour Patch Watermelon. I throw it in the basket when Brooke leaves to go to the restroom so I could surprise her. I pay quickly and meet her at the front, where we make the short walk back home.

When we walk in the door, Brooke immediately takes the DVD from the bag to put in the player, only for her to see the small watermelon candy and shout, "You found them!" while jumping up and down. I grin at her while making the popcorn and pouring some rootbeer into a cup before grabbing some plates and the candy to sit down on the couch.

We spend the rest of the day relaxing, watching the movie and a few tv show episodes before my mom arrives home and orders pizza for dinner for the girls, and I decide to make some pasta.

I'm putting the noodles on the stove when she comes over and hugs me from behind. I turn around and hug her back. *I didn't know that a hug could feel like this.*

"Thank you, for earlier today on the phone" she says finally. I grin into her hair. She doesn't need to explain why.

"Brooke, I could tell there wasn't any malice in that conversation. I think you need to just hear her out tomorrow. Is that something you want to do, or do you feel like you have questions you need answered?" I ask her, trying to speak gently.

She looks down before responding. "I know. Of course, I have some questions I'm sure will come up, but I think that I'm just happy to hear from her."

She hugs me a little tighter now, and my heart flips in my stomach at the action. *What is this girl doing to* me? I hold her a little longer, resting my chin on her head, before returning to the pasta. I turn to the side so I can stir the pasta and wrap one arm around Brooke still. The pasta starts to float, and when all the food is finished cooking, she lets go of my hug, so I grab a strainer. When I finish preparing the pasta, she grabs forks and napkins, placing them in their respective positions on the island while I place the bowls.

We sit down and start to eat our food. It tastes great for

just pasta and butter, and Brooke grins at me after taking a forkful in her mouth, my heart beating a little faster when she does.

When we finish, Brooke decides to read, so I go upstairs to grab her book and we lay in my bed while she reads out loud until we both get extremely drowsy. I lightly tap her to let her know she can either get more comfortable or go to her own room, and she gives me the smallest tired smile before saying goodnight and quietly getting up to go.

I decide to send a text to Andrew and say goodnight, and he texts back quickly. Then, I lay there for a little while longer thinking about the day and how it felt so natural and perfect. I wonder if she felt the same. *Could she feel the same?*

Chapter 8
Before

My body feels the numb biting of the wind outside. For a moment, I wonder if I'm dreaming or if the cold is really there, but when the harsh sting of snow lands on my neck, I know it is real. I open my eyes slowly, seeing that the car door next to me is open. I frown, certain I closed it earlier, but I must have been mistaken.

I close the door, instantly feeling slightly warmer, so I go to fall back asleep only to realize Brooke is not here. My flannel is lying on the seat, along with her half of the blanket she and Lydia were sharing, but she is nowhere to be found.

I move Emily, very slowly so as not to wake her, to where Brooke was sleeping, placing the blanket over her, and quietly open the door again. When I step back out into the cold, I'm immediately hit with the biting wind I'd felt only a moment before.

Is she okay? Did she leave? Was I dumb enough that she led me to believe she was going to wait with us to go to that cabin? Why would she do that? She was the one trying to convince Andrew it was dangerous to go.

I start to search for her. The almost non-existent moonlight mixed with the snow makes everything harder to see. I whisper-yell her name over and over, but no response.

Then I hear a noise rustling the tree leaves near the clearing. Brooke emerges, a surprised and confused look covering her face. I sigh, thankful she didn't decide to make that journey, but also thankful she is okay.

"I woke up with you missing and the door open. I thought you were either hurt or left for the cabin," I say.

She shakes her head. "No, I just had to go to the bathroom."

I nod, feeling the effects of my partial fear mixed with my tiredness.

"Alright, let's go back to the car. I don't want Emily to wake up scared." I extend her a hand to step over some rocks, and she takes it. We walk back to the car and both climb in, and I shut the door behind us. Brooke hands Emily back to me, and when she stirs, I worry that we woke her, but she just breathes heavily. I lean her against my chest once more while Brooke takes my flannel and places it below her head. As she wraps the part of the blanket she has around her body, I watch as she closes her eyes, and as they flutter shut, I feel the heaviness of my own. Giving in, I feel the weight of Emily's little body breathing against my own, trying to match its rhythm.

When I wake up this time, it isn't because of the cold—something is shaking me awake. Or more accurately, *someone.* I startle, looking for who was trying to wake me up, and I see Brooke's worried face. That can't be good. I also notice that the sky is getting darker, a sign that I slept in really late today. Judging from the looks on everyone's faces, they did too.

Lydia is also awake, holding Emily, her good hand stroking the sleeping five-year-old's hair. I look over at Andrew, Andrew's empty spot, that is, and then Brooke, willing her to say something, anything.

"Andrew is gone," she says slowly.

"What do you mean gone?" I ask, hesitantly, not wanting to jump to conclusions, even though I already know what is going on.

"I mean he's gone. He took his bag from the trunk and left sometime this morning. He was here when we got back earlier—I remember seeing him—so he must have left after that. I don't know how long—"

I don't give her a chance to finish talking—I open the door, closing it quietly, and then go to the smashed trunk. Someone had covered it with another towel at some point yesterday, so none of our belongings are covered in snow. I grab two of the tent poles I didn't use and the knife Andrew gave me yesterday, starting to head off in the direction of the path.

"Where are you going?" She starts after me.

"I think you know," I say, unnecessarily harsh.

"Jackson, you're being unreasonable. You're doing exactly what we said was dangerous to do without a second thought."

"I don't really care," I say, telling her the truth. In that moment—be it hail, thunder, or lightning—nothing can stop me. I head farther down the path, slowly lowering to reach the bottom. Some of the rocks have ledges in them, which would allow me to climb back up.

I reach the bottom and continue, but I still hear her following me down the path, so I stop and turn around, asking, "What are you doing?"

She looks at me incredulously as she responds, "Well, I'm not going to let you go alone, if that's what you thought was going to happen." She finishes her descent and brushes her legs off.

"You can't."

"Watch me."

"It isn't safe," I argue.

"If it isn't safe for me, it isn't safe for you. There isn't anything out there that you can handle any more than me." She is right, of course. Unless it's building a fire or something similar, she could probably handle any animal out there as well as I could.

Still, I'm about to argue back at her until I see a pair of golden eyes behind her. Until that point, I hadn't heard anything, but I listen quietly and hear the low growl I was afraid of. I look at Brooke, putting a finger to my lips and motioning for her to come closer to me.

As soon as she reaches me, the growling gets a little louder, and I watch as the two wild dogs walk out from behind a few of the trees. I think back to what I learned as a Boy Scout. Don't show fear. Make yourself bigger. Make your voice louder. Don't run but get out of there slowly.

"Stay behind me," I say in a low and quiet voice.

"Do you know what to do?" Brooke asks me, fear evident in her wavering voice, and I nod.

Projecting my voice as loud as I can, I yell, "We're not afraid of you! Go away, go away! We're not afraid of you, go away!" Then I whisper to Brooke, "Back up with me, slowly. Do not show them you are scared."

We back up, and I keep repeating my saying over and over as loud as I can. Eventually, the dogs get disinterested or afraid, I'm not sure which, and they retreat into the trees behind them. Brooke and I sigh in relief.

She looks at her watch before saying, "It's almost evening. You slept all morning, we all did. We wouldn't have enough time to look for him today even if we went out today. You need to also think about how you didn't pack any food, and all you have eaten in the past two days is a sixth of a candy bar. You haven't drank any water, and you were too blind in rage or fear that you didn't stop to think about everything else going on." Brooke pauses, and then says, "We can climb back up there, prepare to leave tomorrow early, and get some good preparedness for the trip. Don't be stupid. You aren't a stupid guy, Jackson."

I sigh. I know she is right, but I'm scared. If those dogs found Brooke and I, I'm sure they could find Andrew. But he could still be fine.

"Okay. Let's go up," I say, and Brooke agrees, walking back to where we climbed down. It takes no more than ten minutes to climb to the top, and when we get back up, I look out over the area I would have just walked without a care as to what is out there.

"Brooke," I say carefully. She glances back at me, as she had already started walking toward our camp.

"I'm sorry for how I spoke to you. You have been nothing but nice to me, and I just treated you so poorly. I was just worried about Andrew. Still am." I am a little ashamed, even recounting my actions earlier.

"Jackson," she says, reassuringly. "You were protecting your brother. I would give anything for a brother who would walk into danger for me like that. I understand but thank you for apologizing anyway."

As we walk along, I start to ask her questions, realizing though it feels like I have known her forever now because of circumstances, I really don't know much about her at all.

"Do you have any siblings?" I ask her.

"I have an older sister. She's twenty-two." Brooke pauses for a moment. "We don't really talk." Then, as if to distract me, or herself, she says, "What about you? Anyone else other than Andrew?"

"Andrew and I have two younger sisters. They're twelve and ten, so they still live with our mom." Brooke says nothing in the silence that follows. "Can I ask you a personal question?" I say, looking at her carefully.

"Only if I can too," she responds quickly, and amused, I continue.

"You said you don't really talk with your sister. What's that about?" I ask. She is quiet for a little, so much so that I almost tell her she doesn't have to answer.

"My dad was a med tech soldier in Afghanistan. He was a

great man and the best dad, but he didn't make it home after his troop got invaded and bombed. My mom kind of lost her mind when Dad died. She started to drink, like a lot." She sighs. "She partied a lot and ended up married to a bad guy who mistreated her a lot. We begged her to leave him, not understanding how she could stay with him, but she wouldn't listen." Brooke is looking up into the sky like she is searching for something.

"We would see less and less of her, and by the time I turned seventeen, she was gone. I started to have to take care of myself then because Kamri—that's my older sister's name—was in college, and I wanted her to have a normal life. She moved home for a while to help me, until I turned eighteen, and she even became my legal guardian for a while. The closer I got to moving to college, though, the more she distanced herself. We would talk some, but it felt like I was being kept a secret.

"A few weeks after I moved into college, she sent me a text to say she was leaving, saying that she was sorry and that she just needed some time to figure out her life. She said that something had happened that she didn't want to affect me. I've tried to call her, but her number isn't in service, and when I look her up, I can't find her anywhere. I thought she might have moved home, or that maybe she went to look for mom, but since then I haven't heard from her."

We reach the campsite and sit down on the log outside the car. I see Lydia still in the car with Emily asleep. Turning back to look at Brooke, I see she isn't her smiley-self anymore. I can tell that she doesn't like to talk about her family very much.

"I'm sorry," I say.

"Yeah, so am I," she says. "My turn, though. Your sisters live with your mom, but not your dad. Divorced?"

I blow some air out of my mouth before responding. "He was never really in our lives. After the girls were born, he was gone for good. They were so confused because all their friends growing up had two parents, and they only had one, so Andrew and I kind of stepped in. I guess that's why I'm so protective of my siblings.

"Alright," I continue, "enough hard questions. I know we had two classes together last year. Aren't you a biology major?"

"I'm a nursing major on the pre-nursing track," she says.

"Did you choose to do that because of your dad?" I ask, and she smiles beyond me, as though she is remembering him.

"Yeah. What about you?" she asks.

"Psychology," I say.

"Is there a specific reason you chose psych?" she prods lightly, and I chuckle to myself.

"Honestly, I chose it originally just because it was interesting and because it made sense for me as an athlete timewise. I've always known I want to do snowboarding in college and professionally, but I also know that I need something on the other end of that. People constantly say I need a fallback plan when it comes to sports, so I chose psychology. Maybe I'll use it as a counselor or a therapist. Who knows." I shrug my shoulders.

"That makes sense. I considered psychology, but obviously I stuck with nursing."

Laughing, I say, "Yeah, I feel like a lot of people consider it and then get disinterested really quickly."

"I'm interested, but I feel like it would be more limiting to what I'd want to do."

"So, do you want to go into the army then?" I ask, not sure what I expect her response to be.

"I don't think so. I always wanted to go into medicine because of my dad, but not into the army. Especially after he died." She sits, silent for a little longer, before asking another question. "You know what I've been wondering?" she says, peering into my eyes through her long lashes. *How is she so beautiful?*

"What?" I ask, desperate to know.

"What made you want to do collegiate snowboarding?" I almost laugh, surprised by her question's simplicity.

"I've always snowboarded, even as a kid. I got really good at it and competed for my high school, which got me noticed by a lot of colleges, but when I placed high enough to compete in The Junior Olympics," I say, trailing off. "Well, that's when Utah State reached out and offered me a full ride. My mom wasn't going to be able to pay for both Andrew and I to go to a big college, so the opportunity for Andrew and me to be able to go to school together was something hard to want to turn down."

She looks at me oddly for a second before responding, "All of that makes sense, but why did *you* want to do collegiate snowboarding? Or snowboarding in general? Why keep it up?" she asks intentionally emphasizing the word "you". I'm a little taken aback by her question, maybe because nobody had ever asked me so straightforward.

After a moment's thought, I respond. "You know, I don't

know. If I take it back all the way to the beginning, I guess I would just say I loved the snow. A lot of life was uncertain growing up with my dad out of the picture and whatnot, but the snow was certain, every winter at minimum. I used to go out there and just think a lot, and it allowed me to clear my mind. Then, growing up, everyone in Colorado my age would either ski or snowboard, and that's when I picked up my first board. We would practice near the house every day and it turned out I had a talent for it. But it always came back to the snow." She smiles at me, clear that my answer had been accepted as enough, and I sigh.

Brooke looks around us, quiet a little longer. Suddenly, I hear her ask quietly, "You know, if we ever get out of this, what do you think is going to happen to Emily?"

I look over at the sleeping five-year-old and sigh. "I hope she will go with some relatives. She's going to be confused, for sure. I worry about attachment problems, though, because a trauma like the one she has had to go through at five might be okay for her developmentally, but it also might not. And I mean, you saw how she was with Andrew for the first day we were here. She wouldn't stop clinging to him. If he were married by now, I'm sure he would try to adopt her."

Brooke's eyes go slightly wide before she responds, saying, "Really? That's quite the commitment." It's true, it is, but he would do it.

"Yeah, but that is just how he has always been. It's who he is. I think, if we get out of here, though, he's going to do everything he can to see Emily."

If. The word hangs in the air. I don't know why those

words haunt me more and more the longer I sit on this log. Just yesterday I fell asleep more hopeful than I had been the whole time we have been stuck down here. Now I feel hopeless, fearful.

"I hate that he is out there somewhere on his own," I say softly.

"I don't know exactly how you're feeling, but I do get it. I'm sorry you ever have to feel that way," she says, her voice kind and gentle.

"Yeah, you're going to be a great nurse."

She grins back at me, and for a second, I forget I'm stuck at the bottom of a mountain.

After an hour of sitting and exchanging stories, it gets dark, so we decide to eat a bit of the candy bar. Again, I insist Brooke eats my piece, but this time she tells me to eat it so that tomorrow I have a little more strength. Frowning, I eat my piece of candy, which only makes her laugh.

"What?" I ask her.

"I don't think I've ever seen anyone so sad to eat a piece of candy," she says, still laughing slightly.

"There you go," Brooke says. I look over at Emily, who is clearly still hungry, and look back over at Lydia and Brooke mouthing "nuts" to them, wondering if we could give her a little more food. They both nod, and I go to grab a handful from the box. We have been trying to save our food because we don't know how long we will be here, so we haven't eaten them yet, but we just finished our last candy bar, so we don't have much of a choice now.

"Hey Emily?" I ask. She looks up at me, her big brown eyes curious.

"Are you still hungry?" I ask her, but she shakes her head. "Are you sure? You don't have to say no so we can eat more." She slowly stops shaking her head.

"Yes," her tiny voice manages.

"Yes, you're still hungry?" I ask her, and she nods ever so slightly. "Do you want some nuts?" We had been trying to ration the food and keep the nuts as a last resort, but right now this little girl needs food.

She looks at me like I just offered her a five-course meal, bobbing her head up and down too quickly for her small body. I lean forward, asking for her hands, which she eagerly gives to me, and I pour the handful of nuts into her palms.

My one hand was able to grab enough nuts to overfill her two little ones, so her eyes are nearly bulging out of her head after two days of eating only a few pieces of a candy bar. I look over at Lydia and Brooke, seeing their faces also lit up in happiness over Emily's treat.

Then I look at Emily and say, "Okay, you can eat your nuts. Lydia and Brooke and I are going to go right over there to grab more brush, okay? Don't go anywhere."

"Okay," she says with a full mouth.

I look at Brooke and Lydia, both a little confused. I gesture to walk over to the clearing, and they follow. When we arrive, they do start to gather some brush, so they assume I meant what I told Emily, making me laugh slightly.

"No, I didn't actually mean it. I can gather while we talk,"

I say. Then I focus on Lydia. "I'm sorry for running off this afternoon. That wasn't right and I'm sure you were concerned."

She shakes her head before saying, "It's alright. I figured Brooke would convince you to come back one way or another." She gives Brooke a weird look, and Brooke flushes. *Weird.*

"Okay, so tomorrow, though," I say, "Brooke and I are going to go out earlier to find Andrew, and if he is close enough to the cabin, we'll go there. It looked like a four-mile walk, so there is a chance we won't be back tomorrow night if the snow is too hard to get through. Are you okay watching Emily?" I ask her.

"Yes, but what about Lucas?" she says to Brooke.

"Lydia, honey, I'm sorry to have to be the one to tell you, Lucas isn't going to wake up anytime soon. You just need to check him periodically to make sure he is breathing. Your arm is broken, so if he isn't breathing, you have to do CPR with your good arm. Obviously, it's not ideal to use one arm, but it will work in an emergency. Can you do that?"

"I took a CPR class a year ago for babysitting licensing, so I know how to do it. I just don't want it to get to that point," Lydia says with tears in her eyes.

"We are hoping to be back that morning unless we have to be out any further, so you shouldn't even have to worry about that, okay? Just keep an eye on him, and we'll make sure Emily behaves," Brooke says.

I can tell Lydia is a little more assured because her face ceases the tense look it had been bearing slightly. Then Brooke looks at me through her eyelashes. *Beautiful.*

"Looks like we're going adventuring tomorrow."

I smile slightly, knowing she is trying to joke a little.

"We'll get up at seven since enough light will be out, alright?" she says to me, and I agree.

After grabbing enough brush, I walk back over to the fire and light it once more. The tent worked well last night, so we use it again. Brooke checks on Lucas once more while I go find Emily's backpack and an empty bottle of water that I now fill with ice. I don't want to waste our drinking water, especially since even though we had a larger pack of it, we are running low now. After holding the bottle over the fire it starts to melt enough to use to brush our teeth.

We all get our brushes wet with the melted ice, Emily included after I had inspected her bag. I don't think anyone has ever been so refreshed to brush their teeth as the four of us are. When we're finished, Brooke checks on Lydia's gash, seeing it looks much better and wipes it down with some of the melted ice. She rips the bloody part and re-ties the two halves of the bandana so she can re-tie it around Lydia's head.

We all move to the car to get some sleep for the night, Emily again asking to sleep with me. I am sure to tell her before we fall asleep that she will wake up with Lydia because Brooke and I are going to find Andrew. Emily hugs me goodnight and goodbye, and then I pull the blanket around her while Brooke places an arm around Emily's torso.

As Brooke's eyes close, my flannel beneath her head, she whispers to me, "Promise me you won't leave without me."

I say, "I promise," and mean it.

Chapter 9
After

When I wake up at seven-thirty, I am surprised to see Brooke in my room. Apparently, she came into my room thirty minutes earlier but didn't know whether to wake me or not. I see the worried look on her face, however, and I ask her what is wrong.

That's when she begins to pace. I think she doesn't want to show it, but she was insecure about her sister and her meeting. There are a lot of "What if she changes her mind?" and "What if she regrets meeting with us?" kind of thoughts spewing from her head. I try to calm her down the best I can, and while it takes over an hour, she finally calms down enough to realize it is okay to go to lunch.

I get up and grab some clothes from my dresser, and when I turn around, I see she is blushing. She decides to leave so she can also change, and I ask her to meet me downstairs. She leaves the room, and I get ready for the day.

When I finish getting ready, I grab a jacket and some shoes and head downstairs. Which brings me to where I am now, fixing breakfast for one. Brooke told me she didn't want to eat because she felt too nervous, and though I tried to convince her to eat something so she would have some energy, she opted for some tea.

I'm fixing some eggs now while Brooke reads something on her phone. The book my mom got her was quickly finished, and Brooke had mentioned last night that her Kindle was crushed in the accident. My mom said she was going to look for her library card for Brooke to use sometime soon, but until then, Brooke was stuck reading on her phone or any of the books my mom got for her.

When the eggs are finished, I return to my seat next to Brooke at the island. I continue to eat while I watch Brooke read, a hand over her mouth while she does so. It is very entertaining to watch her, so invested in the story on her phone. By the time I'm done eating, she must be able to feel me watching her since she puts down her phone.

"Can I help you?" she asks, trying to sound annoyed, but my grin only stretches higher, reaching my eyes.

"No," I say. "I just like watching you read. You're so invested, and it's incredibly entertaining." Her blush deepens. *How does she make even that pretty*?

"How can you like *watching* me read?" she asks.

"Brooke, I like watching you do anything you're passionate about." I don't add that I could watch her do just about anything and still be entertained for fear of coming on too strong. Still, she blushes almost as though she heard my thoughts.

"Well, I can't read if you're watching me. It's distracting," she says, trying to sound annoyed with me.

"I hate to burst your bubble, but I quite like distracting you so I'm going to keep watching you read, and you," I say, moving her chin to look toward her phone, "need to keep reading."

She rolls her eyes, but she looks back at me, hesitant.

"If I'm really distracting you," I say, "I can go clean the kitchen, but I'll have you know I really don't want to." As I say this, she gives me a look that means she would very much appreciate me going away, and I relent.

"Fine, but don't think I can't clean and watch you," I say, but she shoos me away, returning to her book. I walk into the kitchen, my eyes still on her, and grab my plate from the island, placing it into the sink and starting to wash it. It is, however, difficult to both clean and watch her, so I give in and start cleaning the dish properly.

When I finish, I spray the counter with an all-purpose cleaner and wipe it away. Then I walk back over to my seat and watch her read.

"That wasn't long enough," she says.

"Well, it was too long for me," I say, and she laughs. "Besides," I add, "we need to get going soon anyway, to meet Kamri."

She looks up from her book, confused. "I thought that the place we are going is in Montrose. It's only 9:45. Why do we have to leave now?"

"Well, my mom has the car, so we have to walk, and I figured you might want to be there a little early," I say, hoping to earn another beautiful smile.

It works. *So worth it.*

"Alright then, let's go," she says, a little bit of spirit in her voice as she gets up from her chair. I extend my arm toward the door, and she walks to it, grabbing her coat from the hanger by the entrance. I grab my own, sliding it on and placing my shoes on each foot.

"Ready?" I say.

"Ready."

We walk out the door and I start the map on my phone. It gives an ETA of thirty minutes, and that will give us ten to fifteen minutes in between when we agreed to meet Kamri.

We start down the pathway and walk to the left. Two minutes in, Brooke pulls out her phone and starts to play some music. I give her a funny look, and she returns it, giving me a goofy look as if to call me silly. She then looks back down at her phone to choose the right playlist.

She chooses a specific one, and as it starts playing, she puts her phone back in her pocket, the speaker portion facing up so we can hear.

We walk in silence for a while, except for the music and the navigation. It's not out of awkwardness, we can just exist with one another, walking without speaking, without feeling the pressure to come up with conversation starters.

The walk does take about thirty minutes, and because I made a wrong turn, we accidentally ended up taking a shortcut. We arrive at 10:18, and after a quick glance around, neither of us see Kamri there. We decide to walk inside and get our table, and when we sit down, we ask our waiter to come back once the other member of our party arrives.

As the fifteen minutes pass, Brooke plays with her hands, nervously bouncing her leg up and down. I take one of her hands into my own. As I do, I feel our waiter walk next to us and I look up to see a girl who looks a lot like Brooke, but older, standing behind him.

I look over at Brooke, who looks a little shocked that her sister is indeed standing in front of her. I stand up and extend a hand to Kamri before introducing myself.

"I'm Jackson Carter. According to Brooke, we are bestest friends." I try to throw in a joke to jar Brooke's mind from spiraling. It works, and when she looks at me and starts to laugh at my recollection from the other day. Kamri looks between the two of us and laughs herself.

"I'm Kamri," she says. Her voice is a little deeper than Brooke's, but her face matches Brooke's more than Andrew's matches mine.

Then she turns to Brooke, and she gives her a look that overpasses any kind of hurt they had between the two of them. Brooke stands up and steps forward, taking Kamri into a hug. The girls don't look upset with one another or like any bad blood is between either of them. They're just happy to be hugging, and it only makes me wonder more why Kamri left in the first place.

Then I look behind the two girls and see a man standing behind Kamri. He doesn't look like he is trying to get around them, but rather looks as though he is waiting to be introduced. Sure enough, when the girls separate, Kamri wipes a tear from her eye and puts an arm around the man.

"And this," she says, gesturing to the man, "is Reggie."

But when Brooke looks shocked and reaches for Kamri's left hand, I realize this might be a lot of news for Brooke to take in. I see the sparkling diamond on Kamri's ring finger and realize she isn't introducing us to her boyfriend—she is introducing us to her fiancé.

Brooke, though, doesn't panic out of overload on information, but instead grins widely and squeals.

"What? You're engaged! You need to explain. Sit, sit." Brooke starts to speak quickly, almost as though if she doesn't, she won't ever get the chance. Then, she turns to Reggie and shakes her head. "I am being so rude. I'm Brooke, but obviously you knew that, and this," she says, turning to me, "is Jackson. He is my bestest friend." She grins up at me, and I laugh lightly.

"Nice to meet you," I say, shaking his hand, and when I let go, Brooke leans in to hug him. We all sit after she pulls away and Brooke gives Kamri a knowing look that all but says 'explain.'

"Well," Kamri says, "it's kind of a long story." I look at Brooke and see in her eyes the realization she is going to get some of the closure she has been dying for.

"Two months after I turned twenty, I went on a river rafting trip with my friends. You remember?" she asks Brooke, who only urges her to continue.

"Well, I met a guy on that trip. He was my age, went to the college in the town over from mine, and we partied a lot. I kind of got obsessed with him. It got to the point where I was visiting him almost every weekend when I was at college. He was amazing, and a nightmare I couldn't escape. I loved him, and I thought he loved me, but my friends kept telling me that they saw that he was controlling me. I guess it should have been a sign that I didn't want to introduce him to you that deep down I knew he wasn't good for me, but at the time I was infatuated.

"Then, Mom left, and you needed me, so I moved home and didn't get to see him for a while. When I finally did get to see him, that was the weekend you decided to stay with your best friend." She looks down slightly, almost as though she is getting emotional while telling the story. Reggie puts an arm around her.

"When I got home, a few weeks passed, and I found out I was pregnant." I look over at Brooke, seeing the shock rise on her face. She didn't know.

"I was so obsessed with this guy, and I wanted him to be the father of our baby, but when I told him, he was angry. That night he hit me once, and I left as soon as I could stand. I went back to my apartment and sobbed. I couldn't believe that after everything that we saw happen with Mom, I fell in love with him in the same way. It was like I was watching it happen to me. It was like watching a car wreck. I knew how much he hurt me, how he was going to continue to hurt me, but still, I loved him. And now I had a piece of him forever connected to me, growing in me.

"I knew that if I told you what had happened, you would beg me to leave him. It took a lot of convincing from my friends who guessed what had been happening to get me to finally say the words. He hit me. Those words spurred a whole new chain effect, a legal battle starting when I finally filed a report, but he fought back with brute force. I had never gone to the hospital, so there were no x-rays or documents proving I had ever been hurt, and it was his word against mine.

"That was when I found out that his father was willing to pay for this to go away quietly with an amount of money that I knew could put you through all your school and even after that. All I had to do was drop the charges, move to a new town, and never connect the baby to his son. I knew that if I told you what was going on, you'd tell me to fight, but if I lost this fight—and I felt like I was going to—I would have had to pay for not only my court fees, but his too.

"It felt like an impossible situation, so I dropped the charges, and put the money in your college savings. I knew you were getting ready to move to school, and I didn't want my choices to upend everything you had going for you. You had admission to an amazing school, a plan set for your life, hope for the future. I didn't want to ruin that.

"I had this plan that one day, after the baby was born and we were both more settled into our lives, I would reach out to you and maybe you'd let me back in. It was more of a fantasy built in my fear, but it was something, enough to get me going.

"So, a few days after we moved you into your dorm, I packed everything I owned into my car, and I moved. I picked a random city in Texas called Killeen, knowing no one and nothing about where I was living other than I could get a job to float me for a while at a nearby diner. I had dropped out during the summer term, so I could still transfer my credits if I got enough money to start school again, later." A single tear falls down her face now.

"I sent you that text the day that I left to try to make sure that you knew I wasn't leaving you forever. I wanted to protect you, and I figured that one day I would be able to tell you what happened, but I didn't want my mistake to ruin your life." Brooke grabs Kamri's hand, begging her to continue.

"The apartment complex I lived in was pretty small in a secluded town, and my next-door neighbor happened to be a police officer." She nudges Reggie then. "He lived with his sister, who befriended me and introduced me to Reggie. He ended up asking me out, and when I told him the whole story, he was fully supportive and a bit over-protective." He grins at Kamri, shaking his head in fake protest.

"But I loved it. I felt cared for and protected. We started to get serious, and I started to get really pregnant. When I had her, he was there, and all I wanted to do was call you. I was too scared that because it had been so long, you hated me for leaving. I was worried that you wouldn't forgive me.

"Reggie started to raise her like his own, and even took a leave to help me in the beginning. Then he proposed to me about three weeks ago, and that day I was over at Reggie's apartment; I saw something on the news about a car going over the side of a mountain and there being five survivors." Her voice starts to choke up, and she can't continue.

"They had said it was a few students from a school in Utah, but it took a day or two before I saw your face attached to an article related to the accident. We were making dinner, and suddenly she broke down," Reggie explains. It is the first he spoke, but you can hear the concern in his voice.

"We sat on the floor of my apartment, watching the screen

for updates, and Kamri started to call everyone she knew who might still be in contact with you." He continues to speak while fixing his eyes on Kamri. She has composed herself a bit more now, and she continues in his place.

"I would look you up from time to time to see what you were doing before, but you don't have social media, so it was like searching for a needle in a haystack. I needed to get a hold of you somehow, though. Of course, the news stations wouldn't say which hospital you were at, so it took me a day or so to even find where you were taken to, and when I finally did, they tried to connect me, but you didn't pick up. They told me that you had pneumonia after I begged them and told them I was still technically your legal guardian, and after that phone call, I told Reggie I needed to go to Colorado.

"We packed up that night, four days ago, and by the time we got a friend to babysit, drove from Texas to Colorado, found a hotel and called the hospital, I found out you had been released that day. I figured that I could at least try to come visit you if I could find you, so I did everything I could to find where you'd gone. Eventually, someone gave me Lydia's number and after I explained who I was, she told me to call Jackson's phone or his mom's house. When his cell didn't pick up, I called the house." Her tears are still falling, but her voice stays strong.

"And he picked up, and then I got to hear your voice. I was able to get a hold of you and now we're here," she says, gesturing around the room.

Brooke's smile is still on her face, and I can tell that though she knows the story Kamri just told her is true, she doesn't care. Her sister is here, and she isn't trying to leave her.

"Well," Kamri says. "Say something." She wipes another tear from her eye, looking at Brooke.

"I'm so sorry for everything, Kamri. You're right, though. I would have pushed you to fight. I would have not gone to college and stopped you from being with him. Or maybe I would have continued but switched to law so I could make sure that could never happen again. Either way, I would have supported you, and I wish you would have known that." Kamri's eyes are fixed on Brooke's, knowing the truth behind her words.

"That said, I have a niece?" Brooke laughs, tears still in her eyes.

"Yes," Kamri widely laughs. "Her name is Lila. Would you like to see some pictures? Maybe you can meet her sometime?"

"I'd love to!" Brooke says, and Kamri takes out her phone, showing Brooke baby photos by the hundreds. I watch the joyous look on Brooke's face grow more and more, and I wait to hear her response.

"She's beautiful." Then she pauses, before continuing. "Kamri, I'm just so happy you're here. Thank you for explaining. For a long time, I was heartbroken, and I thought that maybe you thought I had hurt you and so you left. It's just so good to have some closure." She sighs deeply.

"So, when are you planning to get married?" she asks, moving the subject to a lighter note, and I don't miss how her hand snakes under the table to grab my own. I squeeze her back, hoping it brings her a little bit of comfort.

We sit in the restaurant for two hours, exchanging stories, talking about life, and eating some really good food. We learn that Reggie is really into computers, and he tells us the story of their proposal in greater detail. Kamri talks about how she did end up transferring to a community college nearby her apartment and is going to graduate the same year as us since she took less credits a year. Brooke insists that they throw a joint graduation party when the time comes.

When it's time for Kamri and Reggie to leave, Brooke has tears in her eyes. Kamri gives Brooke her phone number, since she got a new number when she moved to Texas and begs her to keep in touch. She also promises that a wedding invitation will be sent to my address, for Brooke and me to attend, after I write it down for her.

Reggie tries to put his card down to pay, but my own card gets to the bill first. We take turns arguing who should pay, but in the end we each pay for ourselves and the sister we came with.

When we walk to the parking lot to see where Reggie and Kamri are driving away, Brooke hugs her tightly once more, and Reggie and I shake hands. They get in the car, and we watch as it drives away.

I get the map out to navigate back to my house, at the same time tugging Brooke toward me and hugging her with my left arm. She leans into me, and though she isn't shaking, I see she is crying.

"Are you alright?" I ask.

She smiles up at me and though a tear falls down her face as she does. I wipe it away from her cheek with my thumb as she says to me, "Yeah. I'm happy. That went so much better than I have ever imagined it would go."

As we follow the map, Brooke talks about how she got

closure, and that felt so good. I mention the engagement, and though Brooke thinks their story is wild, she is happy for her sister.

The entire walk back to my mom's house we talk about the lunch, how happy Brooke is to have seen her sister, and how she can't believe it took a tragedy like the one we were a part of to bring her sister to her.

As we approach my mom's house, my phone buzzes, and I look down to see I received an email from Coach Barrow. I immediately shove the notification away, but Brooke notices.

"What was that about?" she asks, and I sigh.

"It was an email from my coach. I've been expecting it, remember?" I say, frustration in my tone as I do, not directed at her, though. Never at her.

Brooke looks at me and says, "Do you mind if I read it? To you, I mean?" Though I am surprised she'd want to, I'm only slightly opposed. I decide it isn't anything I'm not expecting, so I hand her my phone. She reads it out loud.

Jackson,

I wanted to reach out to you and extend my deepest condolences regarding your recent accident. It is indeed a tragedy, and one I wish you would have never had to suffer. I hope all is well with you and I have you brother in my thoughts and prayers.

I know you have previously committed to competing in the West World Championships at the end of December. I don't expect you to participate, but if you aren't going to, please let me know so that I may give your spot to another member of our team. I hope to see you back on the slopes soon.

All the best,

Coach Barrow.

She looks up at me now. I could have read it verbatim and not have missed anything. It's a nice offer, but if I don't participate, it will mean I'll be pushed to the back of the team lineups.

"So?" she asks me.

I shake my head. "I don't even know if I want to get back on a board yet," I say, but I'm looking up at the sky. Then I look at her. "I need to practice first, see how I feel, and then I can make a decision."

"Tomorrow," she says. "We'll go tomorrow."

Chapter 10
Before

After I initially drifted off, I probably got a good few hours of sleep, but then I woke up thinking only about my brother. It took everything in me not to just get up and go. But I promised Brooke I wouldn't, and though it was just two words, I know I'm not going to break them.

As the sun slowly starts to shine on the snow-covered ground, I look over at Brooke's watch. It reads 6:40 a.m., and though I know we said we would get up at seven, I am anxious to get going.

I go back and forth for a minute on whether or not to wake her, but I decide that we need all the time we can get. I take Brooke's that was wrapped around Emily's torso and slowly remove it from her body, so as not to wake Emily. Then, I tap Brooke on her shoulder, not wanting to startle her.

She doesn't wake up after the first few taps, but after a few more times, her eyelashes flutter open. She looks confused, maybe disoriented, for a moment, but then she sits up slightly and looks at me with awareness in her eyes. I look down at Emily and wrap my arm around her once more. Then I open the door with my opposite hand and push it open far enough that I can get out. I carefully place Emily with Lydia before I take Brooke's hand, and we exit the car together.

Lydia wakes up and looks over at Brooke and I before saying, "Good luck. Please come back quickly." Once Emily is settled against Lydia, I close the door and glance at Brooke.

"I know it is a little earlier than we planned to leave, but I figured we need as much time as possible," I say, but she stops me.

"I totally get it. Let's get our things and then head off."

I am so thankful she is so easy-going with this. That is going to save me.

We head to the back of the car, grabbing each of our backpacks. I take the box of nuts and empty a Ziplock I had some extra pens and pencils in to put two handfuls of the nuts into. As I do this, Brooke stuffs my flannel into her backpack and grabs the tent poles I had brought with me yesterday.

"Just in case," she says to me. I don't even want to imagine what that 'just in case' would entail. Hopefully the wild dogs we saw yesterday were a one-time thing, but I'm not willing to bet there isn't something else out there we don't want to encounter as well.

I cover the rest of our belongings with the towel and look at Brooke to signal I'm ready to go. She slings her backpack onto her shoulders and turns to walk toward the path again. I follow suit.

We walk in silence for a few moments until we reach the clearing, and I stop her before we continue. I want to look over the landscape only slightly below us. She seems to understand and looks in the direction of the cabin as I glance around below us.

"Jackson, the car. It's gone."

My head whips around, looking to where I saw the vehicle just two days ago.

She is right. Though I have to squint to see it, the air is clear enough that I can see the dark cabin, but the car is indeed missing. Part of me hopes that Andrew reached it and somehow got access to the car to get us help. I know the likelihood is low, but he is a fighter, and I wouldn't bet against him. I fear the worst, but I hope for the best.

Once more, I look below us at the path, and under my breath, I say, "You better not be dead, or I'm going to kill you myself."

I climb slowly down to the bottom. When I reach the bottom, I look back at Brooke, expecting her to be higher in the climb, but she's right behind me. I offer my hand once more to her when she nears the bottom, and she gratefully accepts it.

Just as soon as her feet hit the ground, we head in the direction of the cabin. We stay in silence for a while, tension in the air, before Brooke breaks it, trying to lighten the mood.

"So, I'm going to try to distract you from permanently frowning. What are your sisters like?"

I hadn't even noticed I had been frowning—probably from

my thoughts going to the worst of what could have happened to Andrew—but she is probably right to try to distract me. My muscles relax when I think about my sisters.

"Maggie is twelve, and she's the biggest book lover I've ever met, maybe even more than you. She's never afraid to point out the truth but is also the first to notice if anything is wrong. I sprained my ankle once during practice and had to sit out for a week. Maggie decided to fix me pancakes, which were terrible since she was too young to know how to make them, but they were also the best thing I have ever tasted because she made them for me."

This makes Brooke laugh, almost out of adoration.

"Kayla is ten now, and she is the sweetest kid you will ever meet. She once saw a kid who fell off a swing set and ran over, gave him the ice cream cone she had, and waved over an adult, ordering them to get a bunch of medical supplies. She went with my mom to every competition I ever had growing up, and one time when I did a turn incorrectly, I fell hard. She ran out onto the course, which you cannot do, and started to yell for help. I was completely embarrassed, especially when my whole team started mocking me from then on out, but I couldn't stop smiling when I saw her at my games."

"They sound amazing," Brooke says softly.

"They are," I say, and that only makes Brooke grin widely.

"How did you know I like books so much?" she asks me then, quietly.

"I always noticed you with a different book everyday underneath the tree at school," I respond, matter-of-factly.

"You noticed that?" she asks, curiosity in her voice. She

looks down, a rosy blush now on her cheeks from being slightly embarrassed, but that only makes me grin back at her.

"How could I not?" I wonder if she even knows how much of a hold she has on me.

"What are some of your favorite books?" I follow up, trying to ease the slight tension I am feeling.

"Oh, good question," she says thoughtfully. After a moment, she responds. "I think my all-time favorite book is *Looking for Alaska*. There is something about that book that I can't quite pin down, but I truly love it. I think some other books like *Our Town, Alice and Wonderland*, and of course classics like *Jane Eyre* are totally up there, but I love the author's perspective in *Looking for Alaska*." I smile at her rambling about books. It's almost like fresh air for her lungs to be talking about such things.

When she is quiet for another moment, I decide to ask a riskier question. "Do you want to tell me about your sister? Only if you want to," I add so I don't pressure her, but she shakes her head.

"No, I want to." She sighs before continuing. "Kamri is a genius, and I don't mean that lightly. She always did well in school, scoring well above many of her classmates. She was also outgoing, loved making new friends and going to parties." She stares forward for a moment, and I don't dare say anything.

"She was always really good at comforting me. When I was younger, my grandma passed. I was really close to her, so I was heartbroken. Kamri came into my room every night I cried and hugged me for who knows how long."

"She sounds amazing," I say. She really does, and she

reminds me a lot of Andrew growing up. He did a lot of the same for my sisters when they were young.

"She is. I hope I get the chance to see her once all of this is over, but I fear I may have lost her forever," Brooke says, a note in her voice that I'm sure she meant to hide. Hopelessness, and not because of our situation. I want to tell her she will see her. I want to tell her we're going to get out of this, and she can go to her sister. There are so many lies I want to tell her, just to see that smile once more.

But she stops dead in her tracks, looking wide at me. I don't want to look because I fear the worst. I know I need to see it, but I can't will myself to look.

Yet I force myself to look. And I see the dark red tinting the white snow. *Blood.* I feel the acid in my stomach start to bubble, and my throat starts to fill with bile.

It has to be Andrew's—of that much, I'm sure. I can't believe I didn't keep looking for him yesterday. He could be injured—or worse. And I was sitting, laughing, around a warm fire. No, he can't be dead. I have to find him.

So, I start yelling. His name leaves my lips over and over, Brooke's too, as I move forward, following the trail of the blood staining the snow. The words leave my mouth, but I only feel fear flooding my veins. I run forward, farther and farther, pushing my legs as hard as they can go. But the snow slows me down.

I'm so angry now—partly at myself, but mostly with Andrew. I'm angry that he left and tried to find help. I'm angry that he didn't want me to come with him. I'm angry that now he is hurt, and I can't find him.

Blood is pounding in my ears now, and my heart feels like it is about to burst out of my chest. I can't feel my feet anymore, and when I try to keep running, I fall into the snow. I land hard; my hands are shaking. I try to inhale deeply, but I feel myself lacking air in my lungs. I try again, but my lungs feel even tighter.

I know I'm on my hands and knees, heaving and trying to breathe, but failing. Brooke finally catches up to me, but I can't look at her. I can't do anything. I feel like I'm dying. My chest grows tighter and tighter as the acid in my stomach pushes the bile in my throat higher and higher.

This is how it ends. I survived the accident, I survived the fall, but this is how I die? I feel pathetic, worthless. *Does it even matter anymore? Should I just give in?*

But then Brooke drops to her knees in front of me. She takes her arms and pushes me up so that we are both on our knees, facing each other. She then inches forward, grabbing my body and forcing me closer to her. I realize then that she is embracing me in a hug, a tight hug.

"Breathe," she says softly. I almost laugh. It's easier said than done. She repeats it over and over though.

"Listen to my breathing and try to match me," she whispers into my ear. I try to focus on her breath in my ear, but the pounding in my head is overwhelming. Almost as though she can read my mind, she moves her arms so that she is hugging me tight with one arm and massaging my upper neck with the other.

The pounding slows, not a lot, but enough to allow me to listen to her steady breathing. Her hand gently compresses my neck and releases it.

I force whatever capacity of work my lungs have left to inhale, sharply, but still they work. I know my breath is shaky, but Brooke keeps telling me, "Everything is okay," and "Try to match my breathing." It's taking everything in me, but slowly, I start to breathe more normally. My head isn't pounding nearly so loud, my lungs are burning but breathing, and my throat is no longer blocked off by my bile.

I look down at Brooke holding me. She saved me, that much I know for sure. I'm suffering, but I'm not dying. Though she is squeezing her body to me, I am the one clinging to her like she is what makes me breathe.

We stay in this position for what feels like years. The wind blows around me, my knees burn from the cold of the snow, and my chest hurts, but nothing makes me want to let go. My entire being feels like it lives to be held by her, and if I let go now, I fear I might fall.

Brooke hasn't stopped telling me to breathe or hugging me any tighter, even though I know her strength must be starting to falter. It isn't until I actually start breathing at a more normal rate and close my eyes until I actually feel her arms loosen around me. When I do, my heart rate falters slightly at the loss of contact, but not enough to go into a frenzy again.

I open my eyes to see her looking carefully at me as though she wants to say everything and nothing all at the same time. Her eyes look deep into mine, the light blue of her irises piercing my own and searching for something in me.

Finally, I feel my lungs gather enough air to speak four words: "What happened to me?"

"You just had a panic attack. Have you ever had one before?"

I shake my head.

"I assume the fear combined with your tiredness and everything else led to too much pent-up emotion and it all came crashing down just now. You need to get food in your system and rest right now, but I know you're going to argue with me on that."

She's right—I'm not going to rest right now.

"I will accept some food," I say, trying to force a small smile. She returns a small sad one herself and reaches into her backpack to grab a small handful of nuts, handing it to me and waiting until I have eaten each and every single nut. When I finish, I stick out my tongue to prove I've eaten them all and try to stand up.

Unfortunately, my knees have been stuck in the snow for too long and they fell asleep. I immediately crash back down, and Brooke has to help me stand after she shakes her head at my stubbornness. When she gets me upright, I turn to look at her questioning gaze.

"I will rest when we find Andrew, okay? For now, rest isn't the main priority, it's following that bloodstained trail." I know Brooke understands what I mean, even if she doesn't agree with me. I look around for the end of the path I chased before my panic attack, but I don't see it anymore. I look around again and again, sure that if I head in one direction or the other it will show up.

Then I hear a soft moan. It is so quiet that I almost think it was in my head, but then I hear another one. I look at Brooke to confirm she is hearing it as well, and she nods.

My head whips around, trying to discern where I heard the noise come from. Another quiet moan expels itself from behind a few bushes, and I dash off after it, trying to find who I hope I will at the end of the quiet cries.

And when I round another bush, I see Andrew, leaning against a log. His hands are covered in snow and his skin is a pale purple. He looks extremely weak and hurt, and when I yell for Brooke to come, I almost fear that because he doesn't tell me to quiet down, he isn't alive.

Brooke immediately kneels next to Andrew, placing two of her fingers against the lower part of his jaw. The seconds feel like hours as she checks her watch for the time before she says, "He has a pulse. A weak one, but a pulse nonetheless."

He's alive. But then Brooke starts to move Andrew into a lying position.

Without looking directly at me, she must have sensed my confusion since she says, "I need to check for his responsiveness. He might have a pulse, but he doesn't seem to be awake." When he is on his back, Brooke shoves Andrew's shoulder, yelling his name over and over.

No response. My heart rate rises, but Brooke shoves his shoulders one last time, shouting his name as loud as she can, and he wakes up—screaming loud enough to wake the dead.

When I first saw him, I just kept looking at his face. I knew he was injured, but I hadn't really looked at the rest of his body until now. His knee is damaged even more now, obvious by the bruising that is formed around it and the position that his leg is bent. It only makes me wonder how much worse his situation is.

Andrew tries to talk to Brooke, trying to suppress his screaming, but she just shushes him and tries to tell him to rest. He is, of course, just as stubborn as me, if not more, so he keeps trying to talk, but Brooke is adamant. His chest is clearly almost ready to burst in pain, but he swallows it and listens to her. Brooke takes the beanie that Andrew had been wearing and places it around his hands, careful not to hurt him as best as she can.

Then she looks at me, and I know that look. I've seen it too many times recently. While I might be looking at his knee and getting the impression it's bad, Brooke has a better idea of what's going on. She gestures for me to walk over to the side, and I nod, walking over to a nearby tree.

She walks over too, looking at me carefully before she says, "I know you know it's bad. But Jackson, this is truly bad. Lucas needs a hospital, badly, but Andrew needs one almost just as much. I mean, looking at his knee, I'd be shocked if he kept the lower part of his leg, let alone his hands, if we don't get him warmer soon."

She's right—this is bad. I just don't know what to do about it. I look over at my brother, wincing in pain and his eyebrows furrowed to keep him from yelling. Then I feel Brooke's eyes on me again, so I turn to look.

"We need to carry him back, Jackson. He can't walk on this leg, and there is no way we're going to get him to the cabin. We didn't walk far enough."

I know there is no way we can just carry him back to the campsite we made. As a six-foot-two snowboarder, I'm strong, and so are my legs, but Brooke doesn't stand a chance against my massive brother.

"I'll carry him," I say, before adding, "but I don't want to injure him any more than he already is." Brooke agrees and walks back over to Andrew, and I follow close behind her. She finds his bag in the snow, searching for something, then she looks around as though there is something specific she has in mind.

"Jackson, find a strong branch. I'm going to try to set his leg." I look around for what she's picturing. I see a few branches that seem like she described, so I go to grab them. Obviously, it needs to be sturdy, so I find one that doesn't look like I could snap it with my bare hands and bring it over to Brooke.

She takes it and grabs a long sleeve shirt at the bottom of his bag. Then she removes the tent poles out of her backpack that she has placed next to her.

She finds the bend in the tent pole, and I see the rope inside of the metal tubes. I know she is looking for a way to separate the metal, and I realize I still have the knife. Pulling it out of my pocket, I show it to her, and she bobs her head enthusiastically. I lean forward and wiggle it back and forth, and within seconds it snaps.

She now has four pieces of metal from the one tent pole large enough, I see, to steady the knee so she can create a frame around it.

She then looks at Andrew and says, "I'm not a doctor, but I can tell you that if I don't do this, you'll be in worse shape than I can put you in. I need to set it, alright?" He nods, but I can see he wishes that he didn't have to go through it.

She places the rods against each other, framing his knee. When she pushes on top of them to keep them flush against one another, it is then that I see how unaligned his leg really is.

After she finishes framing his knee, she looks at Andrew and says, "Ready?" He nods quickly, repetitively. "Alright. On three. One, two—" She slams the rods on top of his leg, and I hear a loud *crack*. Andrew yelps in pain.

Brooke moves on to the next step, lining up the metal rods again and checking to see if his leg is more aligned. Even I can see that it lines up a lot better. It isn't perfect, but it will have to do.

She then takes the large branch I found and places it on top of his knee and reaches to grab the shirt, tearing it in half. She ties the top of the metal rods with the branch to Andrew's knee and does the same to the bottom. It isn't the prettiest, but it is going to work for now.

After standing up and brushing her hands on her jeans, she looks at me and says, "He's ready." I bend down to pick up my brother, careful not to mess up the contraption Brooke just put together. I place one of my arms under his back, and the other under his thighs, lifting him as carefully as I can. Brooke picks up his bag and we start to walk.

My brother isn't light, and we have some distance to go to get back to camp, but adrenaline courses through me as I make my first steps back in the direction that I assume we came in.

We walk for ten minutes before I have to rest for a moment. Every step that I take, Andrew tries not to collapse in pain in my arms. I hate the idea that I'm causing any more harm to him. I know I need to get him back to our camp as quickly as possible, so I can't rest long.

After a five-minute break and Brooke forcing Andrew and I to eat the last of the nuts, I lift him again, and we keep walking in silence until we reach the path we came down on. I had forgotten, up until this point, that this path was going to be hard to navigate, and staring at it now, I can't figure out how Brooke and I will get him up there.

"We'll work together," Brooke says, as though she was reading my mind.

I let Brooke go first ahead of me, and as I follow her, I feel the burn in my legs. She climbs, and then carefully reaches for Andrew's upper body as I start to climb. We are an awkward mess, but when I get high enough on the path, I can take Andrew fully back into my arms. We climb higher, and Brooke pushes the remaining snow on the ground away so that I don't slip on the steep hill. Thankfully, my feet hold ground all the way to the top.

After we clear the path, I walk him into camp, the light of the day still burning enough that I can see clearly which way to go. As I step back into our area, Lydia looks at Brooke and I with wide eyes, both in surprise and fear when she sees Andrew.

"Is he okay?" she asks Brooke, and while I can't see her respond, I know that based on Lydia's look it wasn't a thumbs-up.

I turn to look at Brooke to see where she wants me to set him down, and she points to the area next to the car. I lay him down and watch as she bends down to check his vitals and his knee. At this point, though, I can't watch my brother's face scrunch up in any more pain, look at Lydia's face as she can see how dire our situation is now, or have Brooke tell me once again with those piercing eyes the truth I know all too well.

"What do you want me to do?" Lydia asks Brooke, and she shakes her head.

"Hand me one of the last few T-shirts from his bag please." Lydia nods at the command and rushes to grab the shirts.

"If you need more help, I am willing," she says immediately, but Brooke again shakes her head and takes the shirts to help his knee be stabilized.

My brother and his best friend need a hospital. They needed it yesterday. Brooke can help for now, but she said it herself: she isn't a doctor, and even if she was, she doesn't have the medical equipment she would need to treat them.

I turn around, frustrated and in need of a little space. I head over to the clearing, sitting down on a log and looking out at the cabin. So far, yet so close. Our rescue, and where I'm going tomorrow. Brooke is going to try to stop me, but so be it. I need to save my brother.

Chapter 11
After

Today is the day that I'm going to try snowboarding again. I woke up this morning and felt for sure that I didn't want to do it today—something about being exposed to the snow once more has been making me uneasy, and I felt for sure that if I went snowboarding it was only going to be worse. I felt afraid of the snow, not trusting it, something I never thought possible.

Brooke wasn't having any of it, however, and bundled into my room, telling me we were going then. I protested as much as I could, but Brooke was adamant, and when I finally took a step toward my closet to put on some warmer clothes, I could feel my body agreeing with the familiarity.

I used to do this all the time growing up. If there was snow on the hills by my house, I would be late to school to go snowboarding before class started. The feeling of the snow beneath my board made me feel powerful, and after getting my snow high for the day, school was more tolerable.

Walking into my closet to find the proper clothing, my mind recalls that feeling, and I immediately start to become more excited to get back on the slopes. I get dressed quickly, even though a lot of the clothing in my closet fits a little looser than it should. Still, when I look in the mirror, I see a reflection I am used to.

"Alright," I say to myself. "Let's go snowboarding." I walk out into the hallway, where I see Brooke leaning against the wall, dressed in warm clothing and some gloves she must have borrowed from my mom.

"Are you ready?" she asks in an excited voice. I nod in response, heading down the stairs to the garage to grab an old board, a mask, and some boots. Once I have all my gear, Brooke and I head out to walk to a nearby slope I always rode growing up.

It was one of the smaller slopes around my town, but it was steep enough that I was able to practice all the time for competitions on it. The hill was small in width, but it stretched long enough that my friends and I would often see who could go the furthest on it or perform the coolest tricks. Next to this hill were another two that had more height, and when we got a lot of snow those were the hills my mom would warn us about. The smaller of the two was where Andrew had broken his arm because he went too fast, and I only started to board down the larger in high school because it was more advanced.

As we approach it, however, the nostalgic feeling isn't enough to bury the nerves I am trying to hide. I keep breathing deeply, trying to quell the feeling, but the pit stays put in my stomach.

"Okay, Jackson, are you ready to shred some snow?" Brooke asks me, faking a surfer accent, and that makes me laugh. "Good," she says. "I like it when you laugh."

I grin at her, and she blushes slightly, though I can't tell if that is from the cold or not.

I look up at the small slope. It's really a bunny slope, so it shouldn't be too hard, but still, the pit remains.

I start to walk up the hill as Brooke cheers me on from the base. I can't be more than twenty feet up, but I turn around and toss my shoes down the tube my mom had a neighbor build for my brother and when we were seven. She had been sick of buying me new shoes when I would leave them on top of the hill, so she built it so I had no excuse to bring them back.

I put my boots on and then I click them into the board. When I look down the slope, I inhale a deep breath, feeling the fear course through me. The snow almost blinds me with how white it is, and what I once found inviting now reminds me of the fear I experienced in the mountains.

I tip the board forward, first very lightly, and then with another deep inhale, I push forward hard. The board glides on the snow, and for a moment the fear takes hold of me. But then the familiar feeling of the snow beneath me kicks in and that high starts to build.

I reach the bottom quickly, and when I do, I look over at Brooke. She is grinning and clapping at me, and I think she knows I want to go again.

I look over to the two other hills next to this one that I

used to snowboard down, and even though one of them is a lot more advanced than the other two, I feel like I can make it on the next highest one. When I make it to the top and push myself and the board down it, the high remains. I feel comfortable again, happy to be in the snow.

I ride this hill four or five times before I'm comfortable moving over to the next one. Brooke looks a little unsure when I tell her I'm moving once more, but she moves along with me, my shoes in her hand.

I climb the stairs that are next to this hill, and I remember the dread of climbing it. It takes a good eight minutes to reach the top, mostly because of the incline, and when I do, I look down the slope.

It's a lot more daunting than the other two, and when I tilt the board forward, the pit of nerves in my stomach reform. I try to push past that and look down the hill. This one is a lot more of a challenge, with rocks and trees in the way, but growing up, that was the fun of this hill.

I take a deep breath, trying to convince myself this is a good idea, and push myself forward. This time, however, I'm unsure as I do, and when the board hits the snow, it lands a little wobbly. I get off balance, but the hill has a steep incline, so I keep going down, my velocity only getting faster.

My nerves start to overwhelm me. When I try to stop myself, however, I realize I can't move, and I start to hyperventilate. There are rocks where there haven't been under the snow, and the ride is no longer providing a high. Instead, it is providing an overwhelming amount of adrenaline and panic.

I can't see where I'm supposed to go with all the snow

flying in front of my face, and for once while I'm on my board, I can't trust the snow beneath me or in front of me. That though only causes my chest to tighten more. I see the snowy ground coming toward me all to familiarly, and the memories of the weeks prior flash in my brain. Gone were the days of blindly trusting the snow beneath my board; I am now afraid.

My board finally slows to a halt at the base of the hill, and when it does, I fall to my hands and knees, heaving for air. I can't seem to find any, though, and I start to feel that moment in the woods again. There isn't anything I can do. I feel like I'm going to die.

Brooke drops to her knees in front of me, and we're in a similar position to how this happened the first time. I feel her telling me to breathe, but I can't hear her well enough to register that is what she's telling me to do. Finally, she gets up, and then I feel a pressure relief in my legs. Then a cold sensation wraps around my legs, and I figure Brooke has removed my boots.

I fall forward more, but she catches me. She tries to search my eyes, but I know nothing is registering back. My throat feels like it is closed, and when I try to blink, everything hurts. The pit in my stomach from earlier resumes its task of filling my already closing throat with bile, and again I feel the sensation that I'm going to die.

Brooke then hugs me tight, as tight as she had before, and while there is some comfort in that, the hyperventilation doesn't stop, and I feel as though I'm going to pass out. She holds me tight, but when she understands my breathing isn't getting any better, she pulls back and looks me in the eyes.

My chest is starting to hurt so bad that I consider I might

be having a heart attack, and as I start to double over, Brooke forces me to stay kneeling.

"Jackson," she says. "Look at me." I barely hear it over the thundering of my heartbeat, but I do. I somehow force my eyes look into her own, forcing mine to stay open.

Then she kisses me. She places a hand behind my neck to pull me closer. Shocked, I blink, my heart in my throat, and then she pulls away, looking slightly embarrassed, but still not breaking eye contact. We look at each other for a moment, our gazes not daring to move.

Then I lean in again, feeling her startled for less than a second, and my breathing starts to slow as I focus on her lips against mine, moving slowly and gently. Her lips are extremely soft, and unexpectedly warm for how cold the air is. Her hands are back around my neck, pulling me closer to her.

We aren't in a frenzy, but instead are savoring each other. It's a buildup of all the emotions we have felt up until this point, fighting to survive together, fighting the urge to feel for ourselves when others are hurting, and finally hurting together to heal together. The feeling is overwhelming, and yet, I need more. Finally, I pull away, and I take a shaky but deep breath before speaking.

"Why did that work?"

"I, um, when I got the phone from your mom, I was looking up things that would stop a panic attack. One of them was stopping you from hyperventilating. I didn't really know how to do that, but I figured that if I kissed you, you would stop breathing or something."

I look at her face again, her blue eyes dilated, her cheeks

and lips flushed, and all the emotions in that kiss hit me all over again.

"Well, it worked." I feel like an idiot. There is so much more I want to say, but instead those were the words that left my mouth.

She nods, and after a minute she stands up, brushing the snow off her pants. I follow her, feeling the cold of the snow on the bottom of my socks. Brooke hands me my shoes, and I take them gratefully.

I grab my snowboard and we walk in silence back to my mom's house. I don't know if it's awkward because of the situation or because after all this time that was our first kiss and neither of us had shared our feelings toward each other yet, but I don't really like the silence. Like at all.

Finally, as we near the house, I say, "I'm sorry. I feel like I made things awkward."

She looks at me, a look of mild bewilderment crossing her face. "If anyone made things awkward, it was me," she says, and I laugh.

"Well, maybe we both made things awkward. No matter what, though, I am sorry for my part in that."

She shakes her head at me. "It isn't fair that you should apologize for a panic attack. No one should ever have to apologize for that." She says this so matter-of-factly that I believe her. "Anyway, enough of that. I think you did a really good job until that big hill. I say we should go back for the next few days and practice a bit more and more each day." She must see the slight panic on my face because she responds quickly.

"Jackson, I could see it on your face that you enjoyed it the first few times on the smaller slopes. I don't even think it was the slope that messed you up but the fact that there were rocks in the snow that made the ride feel different. You couldn't trust the snow like you normally do. You just need some more practice with the familiarity of it all. A few runs on the slopes aren't going to make you an Olympic star yet." She is bizarrely accurate, of course, but then I remember what I told her a few weeks ago.

"You remember what I said on the mountain?" I ask, slightly surprised, but why should I be?

"Of course," she responds. "I wanted to understand your passion for snowboarding, of course, but I probably could have read that on any website. I wanted to know why *you* love snowboarding." Like she did weeks ago, she emphasizes the word "you".

"You're amazing, you know that? I say. Walking a little while longer, I think about what she said and reflect on how I was feeling. I would definitely need to talk with my therapist about this whole thing next time I saw her, but the look I had seen in Brooke's eye just now, like she valued every word I said, made me trust her enough to add, "but just so you know, you're coming with me again next time."

She puts her hands up in surrender and nods quickly, adding a smile to it, and I return it back.

I might not trust the snow like I used to but looking at Brooke and hearing how reassuring she was that I would be able to do what I loved with a little practice and trust, I fully believe her.

We enter the house, and my mom is standing in the

kitchen, bagging up what I assume is the rest of the breakfast she was fixing.

"Oh hey, you two. I was just going to text you. I'm going to Apache Mall to do some last-minute shopping for Christmas. Do either of you want to join me?" The note in her voice hints that she would really enjoy us tagging along, so I look to Brooke for the final decision.

She lights up with excitement, and I say, "I guess we're joining you." In response to my answer, my mom claps her hands in excitement.

"Oh yay! I'm leaving in five, so Jackson, take off a few layers, and Brooke, honey, grab whatever you need."

In about five minutes, we're all ready to go, and we pile into my mom's car again. As we start to leave, I call my brother's room at the hospital, hoping to catch him at a good time.

"Hello, I'm trying to reach Andrew Carter in room fifteen thirty-two," I say into the receiver, and I hear the line click and ring to let me know they are trying to connect me. The line rings six times before I hear my brother's voice.

"Hello?" he asks.

"Hey, bro. It's me."

"Oh hey," he says in a much cheerier voice. "How is living with Mom again treating you?" he says in a goofy voice, and I smile anyways.

"It's not all that bad. Mom made pancakes the other day since Brooke is staying with us," I add, and I hear the groan on the other end.

"Way to kick me when I'm down," he says jokingly, and I laugh.

"Sorry, man." Then I add, "I miss you, Andrew."

He sighs. "I know. I do too, man. I'll be out soon, and I know you're going to come and visit me on Christmas, right?" I laugh slightly, and I hear him join in. "No but seriously, if you don't show up, I won't forgive you."

"I'll be there. Speaking of Christmas, is there anything you want?" I ask him, and he pauses on the other end of the line.

"Well, some socks that aren't hospital socks would be nice, but I don't have anything specific. I hope you'll be okay with some super late Christmas presents this year," he says to me. I smile at his voice through the phone.

"I'm fine with that, and I guess I'll just have to come up with something on my own." I see that the car is pulling into the mall, and I remember that the mall is only five minutes from my mom's house.

"Alright," I say. "I'm pulling into the mall now, so I have to let you go."

"Thanks for talking to me, man," Andrew says, and I beam even though he can't see me through the phone.

"Of course. Anytime." With that, I press the end-call button and put my phone into my pocket. My mom drives into a parking spot and Brooke looks back at me.

"How is Andrew?" she asks me.

"He seems to be in much better spirits now. He knows we are coming on Christmas, but now I have to find something for him."

"I'll help you," she says, and I grin.

After I open Brooke's door and we all start toward the mall, I think about what I'm going to get for Brooke for Christmas.

My mom already told me she is going to get her some clothes, and I don't know enough about clothes to add to that, so I need to find something else. Plus, I wanted to get her something special.

We walk around the mall, my mom separating from us and telling me she will text me if she needs me, and Brooke and I continue walking around.

Brooke suddenly sees a store that she *must* go into, so I follow her in. As I look around, I notice it isn't a store for one specific thing. It's an Amazon store with books that are popular and bought frequently on their app, devices they sell, and more. Brooke starts down one aisle, but I notice something out of the corner of my eyes.

There are five Kindles on display. Two of them are the Fire tablets, but three of them are the kind that I have noticed Brooke carrying around with her on campus. I remember her telling my mom and I that her Kindle was busted because of the accident, and when I see these, I know this is what I need to get her for Christmas, or at least as part of her gift.

I make sure she doesn't see me before I quickly pull a store associate over, asking for their most popular Kindle. It isn't too expensive for a gift for Christmas, so I pull out my card and ask them to charge me while I run next door and grab a different bag.

I walk to the store next door, a clothing store, and hand the cashier a dollar for a bag. Then I quickly walk back to the Amazon store, walking to the cashier immediately and seeing that he has the Kindle in a new box and some tissue paper to throw into the bag. I immediately make the bag look nicer, thank him, and then I grab my card and look for Brooke.

My heart is still racing from trying to keep her from seeing me buying her gift, but when I walk to the back where the books were, she is so focused on them, I doubt she would have noticed what I was doing anyway.

She looks up at me and smiles sheepishly. Just her smile is enough to make my heart flip a little though.

"Alright, pick a book and let's go," I say to her, and she laughs at me.

"You think I'm only going to get one?" she says to me, and I laugh in response.

We walk to the front of the store, and she checks out with her two books. Then we move onto a music store nearby, and again, Brooke splits up from me, but this time I see some guitars that pique my interest.

I have played guitar since I was eleven. I have always had an appreciation for music because of this, and I love a beautiful guitar. The owner of the store has some on display, and those are the kind I would pay thousands for. Just looking through the glass at them makes me jealous, but also amazed at their beauty.

I pick up a few and play a few chords on them. Each has a beautiful sound and each is so unique. The manager walks over when he hears me playing some Luke Combs on one of the guitars and grins.

"It sounds like you know what you're doing," he says to me, and I nod.

"I've been playing for nine years."

"Keep practicing, kid. You've got a talent there."

I shrug as he leaves, unsure of how big of a deal my guitar skills were, but I continue to play for a little while longer. After fifteen minutes or so, I put the guitar down and go to find Brooke.

When I finally find her, she is checking out and receives a slip but no bag. I give her a confused look, but she stuffs the slip into her jean short pocket and walks toward me.

"What was that?" I ask her, but she just shrugs.

"I bought something online that I liked, and they didn't have it yet. I'll have to come back and get it tomorrow."

"Okay," I say, still feeling suspicious.

"Ready?" I ask before she takes my hand and leads me toward the door.

We leave the store and wander around the mall a bit more. We pop into a few stores, but nothing draws us in for long, and before we know it, we've moved onto the next store. The whole time, however, I am wondering what Brooke bought. I ask a few times, and she shakes her head, set on not telling me, which only makes me want to know more.

We end up near the food court after a while, and there is a booth selling gourmet cookies. I track Brookes eyes as they land on the booth and wait for her to look at me for approval. When she finally does, I shake my head and say, "Alright. Which one do you want?" She giggles, jumping up and down like a six-year-old, which only makes me laugh along with her.

We approach the booth, and the vendor lets us try a sample of one of their most popular cookies, the chocolate chip sugar cookie with Maldon salt, which ends up being really good. I ask for two of them immediately, and Brooke points to the menu where I see a Reese's Peanut Butter Cup Cookie. I add two of those to our order, and after I pay, we take a seat at a nearby table before diving in. Something about sitting at this table, just eating delicious cookies with this beautiful girl in front of me just makes my heart feel so full and happy.

We split one of each of the cookies, saving the other two for my mom. When we finish up, both of us feeling quite full now, my mom calls me and says she is ready to go. We meet her at the car, and when we start to drive home, I feel the tiredness of the day already hitting me, even though we haven't been out past four pm. When we get home, I hug Brooke and I kiss my mom on the head, but I announce, "I am going to bed."

As I lay in bed, I reflect on how happy I felt today at the mall. I'd love to just chalk it up to a crush, but it feels like more than that now. The way we interact, the small glances, how I can tell it's her just by her floral scent, her smiles at me, how she knows when I am not at my strongest point and builds me up. *Yeah, I've completely fallen for her.*

Chapter 12
Before

When we crashed, the snow had just begun flurrying around us. I knew it was a bad time to be here from the beginning, but to be here for who knows how much longer raises a fear in me that I didn't know I would have to worry about. The weather still hasn't gotten cold enough for any of us to be completely hypothermic, but every day the fire is getting less and less warm.

On basic instinct alone, I was going to make sure Brooke and Lydia were okay, and when we realized the extent of Lucas's injury, I knew I would have to care for him too, but never in a million years would I have suspected I would have to care for my brother. My twin. He is the one I've always relied on, and now he is relying on me.

That wouldn't even matter as much if I didn't have to worry about us dying from exposure. The cold has been getting a little worse, but I don't think I really realized it because I have been running on adrenaline for so long. We packed for a heated cabin, not a ski resort, and we don't have the right clothes to survive temperatures much colder than what it currently is.

As I look at the darkening sky above me, I am so lost in my thoughts, I don't hear Brooke behind me until she startles me saying, "Mind if I join you?" She peers around a tree, looking at me curiously, cautiously. I nod, and she sits next to me. We're silent for a minute.

"Is he okay?" I ask, fearful of the answer.

"He's alive, but he needs medical help. Real medical help."

I shake my head. Turning to look at her in her eyes, I say, "Brooke, I get it. I know they need a hospital. You're what we have, though, and you're doing a great job considering. I don't mean to put any more pressure on you than I'm sure you already have, but seriously. Don't sell yourself short."

She smiles slightly and nods at me, looking back out at the cabin. I look at her, grimacing as I do because of all the blood. The blood is soaking the front of her shirt, and her hands are slightly stained by it too, trembling a bit. I reach over to hers and pull them to my own, trying to warm them.

Without looking at me, then, she says, "I think you need to talk to Andrew. You were so angry at him, and he needs to hear from you why, but you also need to hear him out even if you think you know what he is going to say."

I laugh slightly. "Why do you have to be so reasonable?"

I get up to leave, but Brooke doesn't follow. She just keeps looking forward at that cabin. I figure she also needs a moment of peace, and at that I leave, walking back to camp.

When I reach the car, Andrew grimaces at me with a painful look before saying, "Hey, little bro."

"You're only two minutes older than me." I can't look him in the eyes though, and I know he is waiting for me to talk. Finally, I say, "Andrew..."

"Yeah." It isn't a question, more of a statement.

"I was so angry with you for leaving. I had a full-blown panic attack in front of Brooke. I thought you were dead, and I was going to die. Then I found you, alive, but you're hurt and not in a way that you're going to recover well from. What were you thinking?"

He looks at me, surprised by what I said, but takes a moment before responding, "I was going to the cabin. If there is a car, there is a person." So, he doesn't know the car isn't there.

"So why are you hurt then?"

"I came across a dead deer, and some wild dogs didn't like me being near their food." He sighs, clearly not wanting to relive that moment. "I tried to climb away from them, to get to higher ground and to antagonize them in a dominant way, but I didn't do Boy Scouts like you did so I must have done something wrong. I fell hard, right after they left, on my leg."

He did indeed do many things wrong. Every wilderness adventurer should know is to not try to dominate the animal but to appear larger and louder as you try to leave. And climbing in his condition was also a horrible idea.

"So, you thought with your already injured leg it would be a good idea to climb a tree to antagonize wild dogs?" I say, almost incredulously.

"I was trying to scare them. I didn't want them to attack you guys. I'm sorry if I scared you or made you worried, but I'm not sorry for going." I knew this was going to be his response, but I also know that he was right to go, just not without us.

He sighs, looking out toward the cabin in the distance. "Look, when I pulled Emily from that car and saw her entire family covered in snow and blood, I was confronted with the gravity of the situation. We are in danger. I mean, Lucas alone needs a hospital. I need a hospital. We all need to be somewhere warmer than this. I feel responsible for putting us on that road, and I wanted to get us home. That's why I went." He looks back at me, his eyes slightly glossy now.

"I know, Andrew." I sigh. "Look, the accident wasn't your fault. Please don't blame yourself. I get why you did it, I really do. I'm just glad you're okay, man." He gives me a halfhearted smile before I say, "Get some rest." I walk back to the clearing where Brooke is still sitting on the log and looking at the cabin, but she hears me and turns.

"That was fast. How did it go?" she asks.

"He said what I thought he would say. But he told me he climbed a tree to get ground on the dogs, and he fell out of it. That's why he's hurt. He also told me that he feels responsible and felt that we were in too much danger, so he had to go." Her face eyebrows rise when I mention he attacked the dogs, then ceding that emotion to understanding. A moment later, however, she sighs a sad sigh and looks away.

I see now that she has been crying, her eyes slightly red and lower lip still trembling. She hesitates before finally speaking.

"We have two injured people, both of whom need more

attention than I can give them. I'm not trying to belittle what I can do; I just know it will wreck me if I can't do something more and something happens. I don't know what that's like." Tears start pouring from her eyes, slowly, and her voice wavers more. "I'm tired. We are in a dangerous predicament. Now I'm crying," she says, laughing despite herself.

"You know you haven't cried yet, right? You have a right to feeling frustrated or scared or whatever too. I mean, come on, I had a panic attack in front of you," I say to her.

"I know, but I don't like not being strong, not being in control." Even though she's saying this, her shoulders are shaking enough for me to know she can't take much more of this. I lean over and hug her to me, similarly to when the car first got hit, and feel her let go.

She cries quietly, softly sobbing into me. And we stay this way for a while, not moving or speaking, listening to the wind. I can tell that she doesn't want me to say anything, because a few times I try to speak, and she shakes head. So, I don't.

Finally, she pulls away and turns to me. Wiping away her tears from her eyes, she says, "Thank you. You're a good shoulder to cry on. Literally." A few more tears fall down her face, and I wipe them away from her cheeks.

"You know, you look pretty why you cry," I say, and she blushes, which is hard to believe because the cold and the crying alone have made her skin more tinted than normal.

"Brooke, I wish I could say that not being in control is going to change, but for now we are stuck here. And I'm going to find a way out."

"Okay," she breathes, but I know she is wondering whether

I believe what I just said myself.

"Are you going to go back out there then?" she asks me, sounding more tired as she speaks. She knows my answer, so I wonder why she even asks, but I nod. She does as well in response

"I hope you know," she starts, but before she can finish her sentence, I do it for her.

"You're coming with me. Yeah, I know."

She grins slightly, almost as though we are sharing a joke and not talking about a possible suicidal trip.

After seeing my brother, I want to leave Brooke behind and just go myself more and more. My worst fear, however, is that she would try to follow me, without me there to protect her from what we know is out there.

Then, Brooke stands and outstretches her arm to me, saying, "We all need to get some rest. You, especially, after carrying your brother in your arms for too long."

I smile, mostly because she sounds like a mother trying to get me to go to bed, and she beams back at me when I take her hand to stand.

I look one more time at the cabin, seeing the snow and descending sunset starting to block it from visibility. The clouds are becoming thick enough that I can't really see anything beyond them, and any warmth from the sun we were hoping for has been completely hidden behind them.

Now I know there is another problem I need to discuss with Brooke. I know she has thought about it too. The fires cannot keep us warm enough if it starts to get a lot colder, especially those who are now more at risk for exposure really harming them.

"Brooke," I say as we head back to camp. "I know you saw the snow and the clouds." She walks a little ahead of me so I can't see her face, but her shoulders are tense as she slows her walking. She knows.

"I noticed it the other day starting to get a little worse, but you and I both know we don't have too much longer before the weather becomes more of a problem than anything else," I say. "Are you sure you want to come with me tomorrow?"

I want her to say she'll stay behind, watch over my brother and his best friend. I want her to say she'll keep Emily safe and let Lydia off the hook from feeling like a nurse and babysitter at the same time.

But I also want her to say she'll come with me. And I hate myself for it. Why would I want her to be subjected to a cold winter, walking in the snow in nothing but jeans, my flannel, a shirt, and a jacket trying to reach a cabin? Why would I want her to be in danger of being attacked by the wild dogs?

The truth is, I'm terrified. I'd go out there right now to save my brother or Brooke, or any of the others, were it not for the weather and the darkness. I'd do it willingly and terrified if it meant they'd be okay.

If I failed, I would never forgive myself. If Brooke got hurt—or worse—I would never forgive myself. But I want her with me. She makes me feel safer, though in reality, I'm the one who should be making her feel safer; I'm the Boy Scout.

But she is my rock. She has been. It's funny how we only knew each other a little before this trip, and now I feel like I've known her forever. It feels as though we've lived a full life together, shared heartbreaks and struggles, the pains of our family disappointing us, but also the goodness of friendship and caring for one another. It feels like this is a forever kind of thing.

And that is why when she responds, "Yeah, I'm sure, you idiot," I smile, inwardly slapping myself for it.

We reach our campsite, and I start to prepare some food and clothes for tomorrow. I set aside clothes for Emily, knowing her little body needs plenty of protection, and I set aside Lydia's bag since she had already been changing periodically to stay warm. Then I grab two of the last graphic T-shirts from my brother's bag for Brooke to use for Lucas and Andrew. I also pull out a shirt of my own from his bag for Brooke to change into and out of the bloodied one, as well as a pair of sweatpants sticking out of Lydia's bag and some of my socks. Then, Brooke walks over from where she was talking with Lydia.

"What are you doing?"

"Trying to find some warmer clothes for everyone. Do you think these could fit you?" I ask her, holding out the sweatpants to her. When she holds them to her small body, I see that they are just a little bit too big on her, but she just grins. I knew she and Lydia were small before we were out here, but Brooke is even smaller than Lydia. Maybe it was the few days out here?

"I think they're too big," she says, but I shake my head.

I point to the drawstring and say, "They might be too big, but the drawstring will keep them up. You need to stay warmer." She rolls her eyes at me, but she gratefully accepts the sweatpants, folding them to put under her arm.

Then I hand her the shirt I had pulled from earlier and a

pair of socks. She gives me a funny look.

"What?" I ask.

"I just think it is funny that I'm going to be wearing pretty much only other people's clothes," she says, and I laugh.

"Well, I think that size-too-big sweatpants, large socks, T-shirt, jacket and a pretty comfortable flannel ought to help keep you a bit warmer," I say. "I can take them back," I add, jokingly, but I don't want to mean it. And she doesn't seem to want me to either.

Brooke walks away to go change, I presume, and I look in the rest of my brother's bag to see if he has any clothes that will help. The bag is pretty bare—almost of his shirts were used, and I set aside some clothes for him—so all that is left is a single T-shirt of my own, a thin zip-up jacket, and some joggers.

At this point, however, the wind biting against my arms and legs is almost as painful as the cold, so I take it and move over to reach the food. There really isn't much, and in reality, the food that is left should go to the rest of the group, so I only grab a few nuts for Brooke and none for myself.

Then I cover our belongings and turn around to walk over to the car when I see Brooke walking over in my clothes. I try to hide my smile, but she looks so different. Lydia's sweatpants fit her well enough, but my shirt is three sizes too big for sure. She put her boots back on over the socks I gave her and grabbed my flannel from her backpack to wear under her jacket.

I smile at her, and then I turn back to the belongings. I cover our things with the towel, grabbing the set aside clothing and food, and turn back to Brooke.

"Brooke, here are two shirts for the guys' dressings. I'm going to change," I say, handing her the shirts I found earlier. She walks over to the car's front, and I switch my shirt and pants for the joggers and my shirt that I found earlier.

I look at my legs, which are very pale compared to my normal tan skin, and I fear that soon permanent damage might happen if we aren't careful. I know that I am not the only one whose legs look like this too, and I begin to worry all over again.

Then I throw the pants and shirt next to the car and put on the new socks, throwing the old ones after the other discarded clothes. Soaked in blood and snow, there is no way I'm ever going to wear those again.

I then pull the jacket I have been wearing off to put the think jacket underneath it, and as I do I feel the cold air bite every inch of my uncovered skin. I quickly pull each jacket on and shiver as I get used to the slight warmth of the jacket.

I walk to the front of the car, looking for Brooke when I see her pull away from Lucas with a look on her face I did not want to see.

"We've got a problem."

"What's going on?"

"Lucas's arm," she says, pointing to it. "I stabilized it, but we didn't have the right materials to keep it completely safe from infection." I see the tears in her eyes, and I know she sees this as her fault.

Just looking at the arm, I can see something is wrong. There is some yellowish-purple liquid soaked into the double-lined T-shirt dressing she used to protect it earlier—this is the infection she feared.

Brooke leans into the car and starts to unwrap the shirts. What had soaked into the makeshift bandage didn't even scratch the surface. What couldn't absorb has started to seep down his arm and onto his shirt and pants.

Then she takes some ice from the ground and places it on his arm, using a bandana that I recognize as the one I used on Lydia's head to wipe away the infection. She must have grabbed it from Lydia at some point.

"Jackson, I know I sound like a broken record, but he is dying." She sighs, and I know she hates not being able to do anything. "This isn't even the worst part," she says, gesturing to his arm. "The infection alone will send him into sepsis, but his head injury combined with him not waking up means he may never wake up, even if we fix the infection. If he has any chance, we have to get him medical help now."

I know she is right, and I know what I have to do. At this point, it is our only chance. In the back of my mind, I have been putting it off in hopes that it wouldn't come down to this. I wanted to be rescued by now. Looking at the intensity in the clear blue eyes staring at me, however, I know that isn't an option anymore.

Brooke is going to try to stop me. I know she is thinking the same thing I am.

"You know what I'm going to say, right?" I ask her, sighing.

"And you know there is no way you are going to that cabin alone, right?" she retorts. I shake my head. *Why does she have to be so stubborn?*

"It's dangerous, Brooke. More dangerous than before."

“I know. What did I say last time, though?”

“I won’t forgive myself if something happens to you,” I say, hoping some part of her wants to stay behind, to listen to me. Yet that voice from earlier reminds me that no matter how badly I want her to stay, I need her.

“Nothing will happen to me. You wouldn’t let it.” And there it is. Any semblance of me that wanted to fight her to stay behind is gone.

“We’re leaving now.”

Chapter 13
After

The past week or so consisted of Brooke and I repeatedly going to the hills to practice my snowboarding, meeting with our therapists for the first time, going to and from the hospital, and playing lots of games.

Brooke convinced me that I could learn to snowboard again without fear and insisted on me teaching her how to snowboard. Oddly enough, I think that her asking me to do that helped me to overcome any nerves I had been feeling about getting back on my board.

She also had made me explain to her why I had loved snowboarding, what the feeling was that I loved so much about it. I didn't understand why until later in my "rehab" process.

Day after day, she would drag me to get up, I'd get my clothes on, and then we would head out to the three hills. She wouldn't let me go on the third hill until I did multiple rounds on the other two, and I got annoyed with her for not letting me do what I wanted.

After I did this for a few days, I started to realize she would purposefully make me get annoyed with her so that when she did let me on the slope, I was thankful to be riding on it finally.

The first time I went down the third slope after my panic attack, I was hesitant, but Brooke had gone through the slope as best as she could to clear the snow, and she told me to keep my eyes on her as much as I could. She kept telling me to feel the board in the snow, repeating what I had told her on the first day.

Once I started to focus on the feeling and not the fear, I was able to make it down with ease and when I reached the bottom, I had a huge grin on my face. I looked over at Brooke and saw that she was matching my smile with one of equal size on her own face.

Day after day, I started to go down the slopes with less tension. I also got Brooke to ride the second largest hill comfortably, to the point where she tried the third hill. Though she fell the first time, she kept trying over and over, and eventually succeeded.

She never gave up, each time climbing up those stairs with confidence that even if she fell, it would still be alright. I loved seeing that, almost living vicariously through it. I wish I had less pressure, to be allowed to feel like I could fall, and it would be okay.

At the end of the third day, I decided to email my coach. I talked with Brooke about it, unsure whether it was the right decision.

After my multiple days of training, I knew that I could compete, but I ended up drafting an email to my coach that said I would not compete. I showed it to Brooke, and she read it out loud.

Dear Coach Barrow,
I appreciate your email and your condolences. My brother is doing better, and hopefully I'll get to see him up and at 'em soon.
I am writing to you in response to your question as to whether I will be competing. Though I believe I am strong enough to compete, I will not be competing with the heart and the passion that the team requires of me. I will continue to be on the team in the coming semester, but I will not be participating in the upcoming competition.
I understand that this may result in a lowering of my position on the line-up, and I am alright with that if it means I get more time to heal, to regrow my love for the sport again, and to feel the spark I used to feel when I snowboarded before.
Sincerely,
Jackson Carter

Brooke looked up at me when she finished reading it out loud, and she grinned. She gently placed her hand on top of mine, and I felt a slight buzzing between us when she did so. I knew she approved.

Then I called my brother and read him the email, Brooke sitting right next to me as I did with my hand in hers and she squeezed it. He was silent as I read it, and when I finished, he was quiet for a minute.

Then he said, "I think that might be the most honest you've ever been with your coach about snowboarding, or yourself for that matter."

I chuckled, and after he gave me a few critiques, he agreed that I should press the button.

Then I brought it to my mom. She read the email, and with tears in her eyes she pulled me into a hug.

"I'm proud of you for standing up for yourself and not putting only half of your effort into what you do," she whispered into my ear as I hugged her back.

"Thank you," I say into her shoulder. We stayed that way for a moment until Kayla bounded into the room begging my mom to take her to her friend's house.

Kayla had been hanging out with more of her friends lately, leaving Maggie at home without her. Within the past three days, Brooke started to spend more time with Maggie. At first, I think Maggie was uncomfortable, but when she realized she and Brooke had a lot in common, Brooke became her best friend. I loved watching the two of them from afar.

When Brooke wasn't helping me or spending time with Maggie, in the past three days she was really only in two other places.

The first was back at the mall, where she and my mom had done another run to pick something up. I assumed it was the item she ordered while in the store.

The other was at therapy—or more accurately, in her room having therapy. Both Brooke and I had started seeing our therapist virtually, as we were planning to continue to see them when we went back to Utah, and we wanted to start a relationship beforehand.

Brooke tended to stay silent for a little while after her therapy sessions. She seemed like she needed more people around her afterwards as well, so when she finished therapy, I was always waiting with a movie and a hug. We both met with our therapist twice in the past couple of days, once a few days ago and once yesterday. I think we will eventually space these appointments out, but they happened to fall this way when we booked them.

I enjoyed my therapy sessions. I felt like I was gaining a better understanding of my reactions from my therapist, and at the same time, I was already dumping how I was feeling on Brooke, so I felt like I kept repeating what I have been saying.

I spoke with Marcy, my therapist, about my email to my coach, and she agreed that I was making a good decision. I also explained to her the two incidents in which I had had panic attacks, and how I had brought myself out of those. I was quite embarrassed, but she was actually quite impressed with Brooke. I was sure to tell her afterwards.

After my talk with Brooke, my mom called me from the hospital to let us know that Andrew was being released to us due to his rapid improvements. We were all so surprised considering his leg had only a week ago been cleared for physical therapy after he woke up, and he had been in a coma. Still, the doctors had said that if we kept an eye on him for a little while and made sure he was nearby, they were comfortable with releasing him.

Since we didn't have the car, my mom picked him up and

when he got home, I rushed outside to give him a huge hug and help my mom get him inside. He was strong enough to use crutches, but still needed some support. Once inside, Brooke gave him a huge hug and helped him settle on the couch where he sat until the girls got home and pounced on him.

Andrew and I got to chat more about everything and anything, and I was so grateful to have my brother back. Whenever Brooke was busy with my mom, or reading, or the girls, however, he would ask me incessantly when I was going to finally tell Brooke how I felt. I would shake my head and tell him to quit it, but he never did. He insisted that people who aren't together don't act the way we act around each other, and I would just blush and repeatedly tell him to stop. One time, he said this while my mom was around and she joined in, which only made my embarrassment grow.

At the end of the week, I received a phone call from Lydia. I hadn't heard from her in a while, so I was curious as to what she was going to say. I had been eating lunch, so I put her on speaker and told her as such when I pressed the accept-call button.

I was answered by the squealing of happiness coming from her end of the phone and Lydia yelling, "He's awake! Lucas is awake!" I almost dropped my sandwich, and Brooke stilled beside me.

"You're serious? I asked her, wanting to be sure before I jumped out of happiness or something, but she just responded with more squealing. Brooke and I joined Andrew on the couch so he could hear too.

"Yes! He's awake and the doctors are telling him he is

doing great, bearing in mind his situation. He's having a little trouble with general movements and thinking right now, but the doctors say it's because of the brain injury. Otherwise, he is pretty great!"

I had let out a huge sigh of relief when she said this, and Brooke did the same beside me. Andrew was sporting a huge grin, and we all got excited over the idea that Lucas might be able to celebrate Christmas with all of us.

We decided to go see him and Lydia at the hospital after that phone call. Andrew had to stay behind but I promised I would FaceTime him in. My mom drove us to the parking garage where Brooke and I almost got out of the car while it was still moving out of excitement.

Lydia had given us his room number, and when we reached his door, we saw her through the glass wave us in. Walking through the door, Lucas turned to meet our gaze. His arm was casted, and the newly shaved left-side of his head had multiple stitches near the hairline, but he smiled at us. That was something we hadn't seen since Brooke looked him over that first day of the crash.

"Hey guys," Lucas says, with more clarity than I expected. We walk over to the side of his bed and each take turns hugging him lightly.

"Lucas, I'm so glad you're awake. I've missed you, and I know Andrew's missed you," Brooke says.

"Yeah, Lucas, I can't tell you how relieved I am that everyone, for the majority, is okay. How are you feeling?" I ask. I pull out my phone and dial Andrew up, who picks up immediately, while he starts talking.

"Hey bro! Well, I feel alright for just coming out of a coma and everything else we just went through. Lydia was just filling me in. Because she isn't family, they couldn't tell her exactly how I was doing, but I woke up really early this morning, and they called my parents at their hotel." He pauses, clearly trying to take his time to focus on his words, as there is slight difficulty to him speaking. Lydia notices and steps in.

"They flew in after the crash, so they were nearby and ran in. When his mom thought I would be awake, she gave me a call, and I called you guys." I remember my mom telling me that his parents had flown in, and she had run into them at the hospital, so this didn't come as a surprise.

He continues to talk for a little while intermittent with Lydia, and we all sit down to be with him for a while. We were all so grateful to be here.

Which brings me to where I sit on my bed staring at the gifts I had purchased for Christmas. I had bought my mom a set of new ceramic bowls for cooking back around Thanksgiving and left them in my closet, thankfully, to save space and so I wouldn't forget them. A store near her house had new serving bowls and platters that were nicely decorated, and in a fashion that I know my mom will love.

Brooke's Kindle is wrapped in a gift bag that I had found, and next to it are the pairs of socks I asked my mom to pick up when she went back to the mall for Andrew since he had mentioned he was dying for some socks that didn't have grips on both sides. I hadn't had time to get Lucas a gift, but I promised him when we left his room the other day that I would get him one when we get back to Utah. For my sisters, I had my mom grab my pick-up purchases from the mall: a rabbit stuffed animal for Kayla and two new books for Maggie.

It can't be later than 7:00 a.m., and yet I'm nervous to give everyone their gifts. When I was eight, I had gathered enough of my allowance to purchase everyone in my family a small gift for Christmas, and ever since then I've done it every year. Each time, I wake up extra early, excited for them to open my gifts and see their reaction.

Even now, on an unconventional Christmas, I am still anxious, but I think that is because of Brooke. Her gift is kind of two parted, but I'm not sure I'll be able to follow through on it. I decide to try to put that to the side, practicing the breathing technique that Marcy had taught me to calm my heart rate. Oddly enough, it works, even though I never thought something like that would.

I sit on my bed, waiting to hear someone else awake, and finally I hear feet walking on the wooden floor. They stop in front of my door, and it opens slowly. Brooke peeks in, and when she sees that I'm awake, she comes in and shuts the door behind her.

She sits in her spot on my bed, and I look at her. We stay silent for a little while, just being with each other.

"Merry Christmas, Jackson," she whispers to me.

"Merry Christmas, Brooke." It's odd to be spending it with her, but nonetheless, I'm grateful to have her here. Oddly, there isn't anyone else I'd rather have.

Then I hear my sisters rushing into my mom's room yelling, "It's Christmas!" That's my cue to head downstairs. Brooke follows me as I grab my gifts, and we make our way down.

My mom, with sleepy eyes, walks down with my two sisters, sitting on the chair opposite the couch Brooke and I sit on, and lets the two girls have free reign with opening their gifts. Andrew, who has been sleeping on a blowup mattress next to the couch, sits up and props a pillow behind him.

After they open every present but mine, I hand my sisters their gifts, watching as they tear through their bags. Maggie smiles widely when she sees I've picked out two books I heard her talking about wanting to read the other day, and Kayla squeals as she sees the stuffed rabbit. Both walk over to me and give me a large hug. That is the only gift I'll ever need from them.

Then my mom insists Brooke, Andrew, and I open the gifts she had purchased us. Brooke, at first, complains that my mom didn't need to get her anything, but when she opens the box and sees the matching set of a shirt and flowy pants from some beachy-bohemian brand, she stands and walks over to my mom, hugging her tightly.

"Thank you so much," she says.

"Of course, honey. You deserve a Christmas like everyone else."

Andrew opens his gift, which includes new sweatpants and an incredibly soft t shirt. He beams and thanks her as she leans down for a hug. Then, I open my own gift, seeing that she had purchased me a new mask and goggles "for when I get back into snowboarding," as the note says. I also stand, hugging my mom and thanking her for her gift. Then I hand her my own, and when she sees the pans her eyes light up.

"Thank you, Jackson! These will be great for dinner

tonight." She hugs me again, and I sit back down on the couch.

I hand Andrew the small bag with the socks in them, and he laughs when he opens the gift. "Seriously, these are going to be so nice to have. Thank you, bro." I stand to hug him before sitting back down next to Brooke.

The two girls have no more gifts to open, so they start to play with what they opened this morning. My mom helps Andrew up and into the kitchen where she gets to work making French Toast and he starts the hot chocolate. Then I turn to Brooke.

"And last, but not least," I say, handing Brooke her gift. She smiles at me and pulls a box out from behind the couch.

"For you," she says, and I shake my head.

"You didn't have to get me anything," I say.

"You got me a gift. You didn't have to get me anything," she points out and I shrug. "You have to open mine first, though," she adds, and I roll my eyes.

My eyes move to the small box in front of me. I take the box cutter and slice the sides. Then, I open the flaps, look inside, and see that there is a cassette case with a tape inside of it.

I pull the tape out, looking at it skeptically before I observe the back of the case closer. The picture is of a man snowboarding, but when I look closer, I see that it is actually me. The photo looks like it was taken of me on the smallest hill, maybe on the first day we went out to practice, and I look up at her, confused.

"Is that me?" I ask, and she beams.

"Just look more at it," she says, so I do.

I flip the protector over and see the list of songs. None of them are by the same singer, so I am further confused, and when I look back up at her she rolls her eyes, deciding she will explain.

"I got you a custom cassette, a physical playlist of songs that I feel describes our relationship or friendship or whatever this is," she says, gesturing between the two of us. I smile, flipping the tape over.

It's titled *We Aren't Done Surviving*, and the songs on the actual cassette are a bit thematic in their meaning and yet their genres and fanbases were completely different to each other. I realize that she got me a gift that connected me to her. We bonded over her playlists originally, and now I have one of my own.

"What was it that you said on that day? You only make playlists for the people who mean the most to you and that you know well enough?" I smile, thinking that she believes she knows me enough to craft such a special gift, and she pulled it together in the matter of twenty minutes. She blushes slightly.

"I also have the playlist on Spotify," she adds, "but I thought it would be cooler to put it on a cassette than give you a link to a Spotify playlist, especially since you have an actual cassette player." I would have thought it was cool no matter how she made it, but the fact that she thought about this gift for me makes my heart soar.

"Brooke, thank you so much. I love it, truly," I say to her, meaning it with every part of me. She smiles widely, and then turns to her gift.

"My turn," she says, and I lean back slightly, feeling like I got a lesser gift.

She removes the tissue paper out of the bag and looks inside. Then she pulls out the wrapped box, looking at me curiously, and slowly undoes the wrapping paper. Then, when she sees the front of the box, she looks at me with an even bigger smile and leans forward to hug me tightly.

"Thank you!" she says it with so much gratefulness in her voice.

"Open the box I say," chuckling at the happy look on her face. She does as instructed and sees the login information I had set up written on a sticky note, and when she logs into the device, she sees the books I downloaded.

"*Jane Eyre, Our Town, Looking for Alaska, Alice and Wonderland*—you remembered my favorite books! Jackson, I love it so much." She looks up at me with slightly glossy eyes. One would have thought I got her the cassette. She hugs me once more, and I put my head on top of hers as she relaxes into me. This, right here. This was the ultimate gift.

My mom interrupts the moment by announcing the food is ready, and I look at Brooke to ask if she's good to go. Brooke gives her a thumbs up, and we walk over to the table, setting it up for breakfast. I grab all the plates and place them on the placemats Brooke laid out. She also grabbed napkins and utensils, and when we are all ready, we sit down.

Before we can dig in, however, there is a knock at our front door. I frown—we aren't expecting company but walk to the door and open it anyway. Then my smile returns, and I rush forward to hug the girl in front of me.

Lydia is standing on the other side of the door, Emily holding her hand, and as I squeeze Emily, Brooke sees her in the doorway.

"Emily!" she exclaims and runs over to hug her as well. Emily starts to laugh lightly, and Lydia looks over at my mom.

"Hi, Ms. Carter. Sorry I didn't call, but I was wondering if you had enough breakfast for four more people?" I look behind her when she says four, since I only saw Emily and her initially, and I see two other people standing behind Lydia, a man and a woman. "These are Emily's foster parents," she says, pointing to the couple.

My mom grins, and because she always makes enough for a king's feast, she says, "Come on in. We have plenty of food for you four." When Lydia walks in, Emily lets go and walks over to Andrew's outstretched arms and hugs him.

"Lydia, how did you," Brooke starts to say, but Lydia stops her. I was able to get in contact with her caseworker since my mom used to work in this district and her foster parents were more than happy to let her spend Christmas with us. They don't have any family of their own, so I invited them. I hope that is alright." Again, my mom welcomes them into our home, and we shake hands as Emily talks with Andrew more.

After everyone is introduced and we find a few more chairs to put around the table, Brooke grabs more utensils and placemats while I fill some plates with food, and together we set a place for them.

"Yum!" Emily says, eyeing the food, and we all laugh.

After we're all situated, we dig in. The food is unsurprisingly delicious, and while we all sit and talk about how good the food is and the day we have ahead of us, I realize how lucky I was to be rescued, not just to live, but to be with my family.

After we finish breakfast, Brooke pulls me aside. "Kamri texted me that she wanted to FaceTime with me. Do you want to sit in?" Her eyes are innocently wide, and my heart beats faster at the thought that she even thought to ask me.

"I'd love to Brooke," I say, and as soon as I do I see a grin stretch across her face.

"We're going upstairs for a second," I yell to my mom, and Andrew looks back at me and smirks. I shake my head out of embarrassment, but Brooke tugs on my hand so I walk out of his line of vision.

"We walk into my room and sit on the bed, Brooke cross-legged while she pulls out her phone and dials Kamri's number. The phone only rings twice before her phone connects and we see Kamri smiling at us.

"Hi you two! Want to see Lila?" she says, and Brooke immediately laughs lightly, bobbing her head up and down.

"Hi Kamri! Let me see my niece," she says, and I grin at her. The picture on the phone moves around until it finally settles on a sleeping sweet baby girl's face. Brooke absolutely melts when she sees her, and she leans against me. I love that Brooke gets to experience this, especially since she isn't with Kamri right now.

We had talk about whether she should go visit Kamri for Christmas a few days ago, but Brooke felt that unless she was intruding on us, she didn't want to be separated from everyone just yet. My mom was fully onboard with her continuing to stay with us, as was I.

Kamri takes Lila's hand and makes it wave toward us, all while saying, "Hi Aunt Brooke." A small tear falls from

Brooke's eye, and I wipe it away for her. She looks at her niece with so much love, it could almost make you jealous. Okay, so I'm jealous—sue me.

Then the camera turns around and Kamri says, "Okay, so Brooke. I have a question for you." Brooke cocks her head slightly in confusion, and Kamri says, "Don't worry. I think you'll like it. Can you read what Reggie is holding up?" The camera pans to Reggie holding a decorated sign.

Brooke squints because the camera quality is a little grainy at first, but when it focuses, she slowly reads, "Will you be my maid of honor?" the emphasis on the words becoming more excited as she nears the end of the question. "Oh my gosh, yes, I'd love to!" she practically shouts, bouncing on the bed and making me laugh.

"Okay great," Kamri responds. "I was pretty sure you'd say yes, but I'm a little relieved not going to lie." She looks over at Reggie who grins at her and motions toward the side of the phone with his head, and she looks back like she remembered something.

"And Jackson, Reggie wanted to know," she tees up his sentence for him.

"If you would like to be one of my groomsmen?" he finishes. Brooke looks over at me, bouncing a little harder now while gripping my bicep, which only makes me laugh more.

"Are you sure man? I'd love to, but I don't want to take someone else's place," I say, not wanting to step on toes.

"Jackson, you have done so much for Brooke, and I don't anticipate you not being around much longer, so I'd love for you to be standing next to me," he says, a grin on his face.

"Plus," Kamri adds, "now you have to have an official date." She smirks at the comment, and I feel a blush rise in my neck, my face getting hotter. Brooke also looks slightly embarrassed when I glance at her.

Still, the couple laugh together through the phone. "We're kidding. Sort of," Kamri adds.

"Alright, well thank you and I would love to be one of your groomsmen," I say, trying to direct the flush in my face to anywhere else.

"Okay, enough of that, show me my beautiful niece one more time before we have to go," Brooke says, and Kamri picks up the phone to show Brooke the sleeping baby. A minute or so later, we say our goodbyes and hang up, sitting in silence for a few seconds.

"Well, that was a little embarrassing," I say, and Brooke starts to laugh.

"Just a little," she says, but then she goes quiet like she is in thought. I am about to speak to try to ease the tension, but she beats me to it before adding, "Jackson, can I ask you a question?" I get a little nervous when she says this, but I nod anyways because I am curious to know what she is thinking.

"I know that the accident caused a lot of emotional damage and change, and that because of the proximity between us we have had a lot more time to get to know one another, but I need to ask, what is this? What are we doing? I mean, half of the time we are acting like we're already dating. I know that's what Kamri and Reggie meant. And I know that our kiss was more of a save-you-from-a-panic-attack thing, but I can't help but wonder," I stop her from her rambling by putting my hand on top of hers and squeezing, and she looks down to where our hands are joined, then back up at me.

"What do you want this to be Brooke?" I decide to say, inhaling deeply before taking a leap of faith. "I can tell you that without you on that mountain, I wouldn't be here right now. My brother and everyone downstairs wouldn't be here right now. I think you are so strong." She shakes her head, but I continue. "Seriously, Brooke. But not only are you strong. You are incredibly beautiful and smart and funny." I feel the panic starting to rise in my chest as she starts to look me deeper in my eyes, but I shove it down, desperate to continue.

"I love having you around every day. It lights up my morning when I see you, and whenever I see you smile. And when I see you hurting, I can't bear it. All I want to do is be the one making you happy every day. I want to see you every morning and have my day and yours be better because of it." My breath comes out shaky now. "And I'm terrified of this because I don't want to lose you. It would break me. That's how much of a hold you have on me. You have from day one. Everyone saw it but you, apparently."

"What?" she asks quietly. "What do you mean?"

"Andrew called my feelings toward you, 'painfully obvious', and I was worried that because you didn't feel the same, I was going to make you feel weird, so I have been trying to distance myself, but Brooke," I say, grabbing our clasped hands now with both of mine. "I can't do it. You mean too much to me now, and I don't think you feel differently. I," my sentences cuts off when I catch myself about to say something powerful.

I love her.

"Brooke, I love you. I know it might be far too soon to be saying this, and we aren't even together, but it's true. I don't just have feelings for you—I love you. I want to be with you.

My heart is beating a million times an hour. I need her to respond before I faint from the blood pounding in my ears and my chest tightening from the words I can't take back.

"Jackson, you have been *my* rock," she finally says. "I had no family to turn to after the accident, and you took me home with you in a heartbeat. The love your family has given me is so reflective of the love you have shown to me. Even when I did find my blood family, you were more than willing to stand by my side. But not only that, on the mountain you were the only thing separating me from shutting down and fighting. You said that I am the reason everyone is here, but that's not true. You stepped up when no one else could. You are a leader."

"And I love you too. I think I've loved you since the day I saw you with your sisters, or maybe it was when we first kissed. It doesn't matter, though, because I know as sure as I know that we are alive. I love you." Those three words changed everything. As soon as they left her lips, an abundance of joy floods out of me, and a smile that I cannot contain stretches across my face, and hers. I love her. *She loves me.*

"I'm going to kiss you now, for real," I say, leaning in to cup her face, and her grin stretches even wider. Our lips touch, and this time the emotional power of the kiss is overwhelming. I feel her smile against my lips, and I return it. I can feel every molecule of her lips on mind, all the sensations firing in my brain, on my hands, between our lips. If this is how it feels to be in love, I don't ever want to stop. This is a soul stirring, sense heightening, completely selfless act love between us. I can smell the rose-like scent of her hair even stronger now, and the feel of her cheek beneath my hand is like silk. I never want this to end.

Still, I pull away feeling so overwhelmed with emotions, and when I do I take both of my hands to meet her face with mine. Her eyes are just as dilated, if not more, than last time, and a blush is evident on her face. My grin from earlier returns, and she returns a shyer one back.

"I need to show you something," I say, when my brain starts functioning again. "I'll be right back, okay?" She nods to my question, and I quickly get up and run downstairs to grab her Kindle, now knowing that the second part of her gift would be much easier to give to her. Andrew smirks at me once more, but I can't stop smiling anyways. I dash back upstairs, and when she sees her Kindle, she gives me a slightly confused look.

"Hold on," I say, grabbing a sticky note and scribbling something down. When I'm finished, I sit back down on the bed.

"You told me how much you loved *Looking for Alaska*, so when I downloaded it onto your Kindle, I started to read it so I could understand what you loved about it. I noticed a line, and I wanted to ask you a question, okay?" I ask her, knowing she was still confused.

I hand her the Kindle and say, "Open the book and go to the bookmarked page. Read the highlighted words out loud." She quickly opens the device and follows my instructions, and when she reaches the page, she smiles so widely that my heart feels like it's going to burst out of my chest. "What does it say?" I ask.

"Do you want to be my girlfriend," she giggles. Then she bounces on the bed, still cross-legged, and stretches her arms around my head. "Yes, please," she laughs, reciting what Lara responds with. I hug her then, pulling her closer to me, just wanting to revel in the moment. When she hugs me back, I feel complete.

"Merry Christmas, Brooke," I whisper into her hair.

"Merry Christmas, Jackson."

After a minute or so, I hear a knock on the door who I assume is my mom, and I shout, "Come in." She peers around the door, confirming my suspicion, and Brooke leans her head on my shoulder.

My mom smiles at us, rolling her eyes lightly and says, "Do you want to go see Lucas. We are all heading out in twenty minutes or so, to give some time to get changed." I look over at Brooke who grins and bobs her head, and look back at my mom in agreement.

"Alright, well you two lovebirds get ready to go and we'll see you downstairs in twenty." I grab a pillow to chuck at her lightly, and a melodic laugh leaves my girlfriend's mouth.

My girlfriend.

We both get up to go change, Brooke returning to her room, and when we are all ready to go, Brooke, Andrew and I pile into my mom's car with Brooke and I in the back. Andrew felt good enough to come with us, so we made sure to make his trip a little easier by putting him up front. Lydia drives with Emily and her foster parents, and my sisters decide to stay home.

When we finally arrive at the hospital, we spend the majority of the next few hours with Lucas. Emily doesn't stay too long since her foster parents need to return home, and I tell Lydia she can drive with us. Lucas wasn't around for much of Emily's part in the mountains, so he doesn't really remember her, but despite that, she is so happy to see him.

After we say our goodbyes, Lydia pulls Brooke aside as we walk toward the car, and I can tell that whatever she said to her makes Brooke flush. When we get in the car, I ask her what Lydia had said and she flushes again.

She whispers in my ear, "She wanted to know when I was finally going to get together with you," and I laugh in response.

"Did you tell her?" I ask quietly, and she slyly grins. "I hope you know all the teasing that is about to ensue from Lydia and Lucas now," I whisper back.

"You mean you haven't told Andrew yet?" she asks, smirking. She's right, of course. I had pulled my brother aside at the hospital and told him, to which he had said 'it was pretty clear based on my face this morning'. My brother will also be teasing us, but I know that all three of them will be doing it only out of love.

"Fair enough," I say in response, putting my arm around her and tugging her to me. She snuggles against my chest, and I see Lydia next to me laugh and Andrew in the rearview mirror smirk. I don't care, though. I'm happy.

My whole life used to be about snowboarding, but I hadn't realized that snowboarding didn't have to be all there was. Because of my friends, family, and surviving the accident, I have a better understanding of what I want—a home and a purpose. I found that with these people. I'm not going to give up snowboarding, but I realized I needed to prioritize first, and that is starting now.

Just because I have survived the accident, however, doesn't mean I'm done surviving life. I'm still going to have anxiety and panic attacks because of the accident, and I'm learning to navigate that. I'm still going to have nightmares and memories haunting my nights. But I have my family. I have Brooke. I'm a survivor. I'm still surviving.

Chapter 14
Before

As Brooke and I are grabbing the last of our things for our trek, I know that nothing in that woodland or the pain of the growing cold could be more torture than losing my brother, my twin.

Brooke is trying to be rational, but I can tell she's scared. The past ten minutes, as I try to prepare the camp for the incoming storm, Brooke has been trying to reassure Lydia of her ability to watch Andrew and Lucas, but I can tell her confidence can only go so far.

I had already instructed Lydia how to keep the fire going, and I decided I was going to leave the lighter with her just in case. Brooke agreed with me that if the fire went out, it would be more dangerous for the injured than us.

As I finish setting up the fire, Emily walks up to me. When she approaches me, I can tell she knows something is wrong.

"Are you leaving again?" she says as her lip quivers, making the annunciation of her words wobblier than the normal five-year-old.

"Yes Emily," I say, and tears spring to her eyes.

"Are you going to my Mommy and Daddy?" she says, clearly trying to hold back her tears. I shake my head, bending down to pick her up in my arms into an embrace. She digs her little hands into my shoulders, letting her tears fall now that she has some comfort.

"Emily," I say as she continues to cry, "I'm going to come back, and so is Brooke." I know I shouldn't make a promise I can't guarantee, but at this moment, I need her to not be scared.

I pull her away from me so she can look at me when I say, "Emily, there is a snowstorm coming, and it's going to get really, really cold. You're going to go with Lydia and stay in the car until we get back, okay? You're going to have to be really brave. Can you do that for me?" She nods slightly, but tears still fall from her clear eyes.

She is trying to be brave. It hurts that I know she doesn't understand what is going on. It hurts that I can't protect her. All I can do is pray that she, and everyone else stuck here, is going to be okay. I put her down and stay at eye level, trying to reassure her.

Lydia walks over to us and says, "Okay Emily, sweetie. Why don't we go over to the car and sit inside? It's a little warmer in there, okay?" I toss Lydia the lighter which she catches, and after she takes Emily, I go find Brooke in the clearing. My nerves build. This is it—the time to venture into the unknown.

She must have heard me coming since she says over her

shoulder, "The car might be gone, but they have to have something to send a signal, right?" She asks so hopefully that all I want to do is tell her yes, that we will be able to call everyone we need to and that we will be alright.

Truthfully, I don't know. I can't imagine there are too many cabins up there, and the likelihood of a flare or something being there when no one is feels too unlikely.

The way she is looking at me now, though, is so hopeful that before I can stop myself, the words, "I'm sure there's something," leave my mouth. *Traitorous mind.*

Her smile is a bit brighter now. I'm glad I get to see it still, even if it is because of a lie. I'm not sure of anything—if I'm going to come back to Emily, if Brooke and I will find the cabin to be full of what we need. But I am sure I'll die trying.

With that, we leave. We move quickly, trying to avoid attracting animals and at the same time trying to get to the cabin as fast as possible. Walking into trees during the kind of storm we're experiencing in the daytime would be a feat. Walking in at night is a trap we laid for ourselves.

We start walking down the trail and into the trees. The cold air brushes against my neck, a shiver being sent down my spine. I know I'm cold, and I know Brooke must be too. My flannel is thick and lined, so she might be a little warmer, but the chill of the wind is still quite strong.

Somewhere along our start into the wooded area, I get lost in my thoughts. I don't remember how long we've been out here at this point. Four or five days seems about right, but I'm dehydrated and haven't been eating enough, so that's feeding my brain fog.

I was supposed to drive to my mom's on the fifth day of us being back in Colorado. Will I ever get to see them again? If I do, will they get to see their other son? I start to spiral, and I don't even realize I'm crying until Brooke taps me on the shoulder and gives me a worried look.

"Jackson, you're crying," she says. So we pause, and I start telling her how I am feeling.

"I'm worried. This is dangerous, what you and I are doing, but even if we're successful, who's to say they can save Lucas or Andrew? Who's to say Emily isn't going to go into a terrible home? At what point does something happen that makes all of this okay?" I know that I sound angry. I am.

"I don't know," Brooke says honestly. "The truth is, there is no way to know, and that is the worst part. There's nothing you or I or anyone else, for that matter, can do to assure you or guarantee that something good will come of this. That something will make all of this okay." She sighs deeply before continuing. "But we have to try to do what we can. So I'm going to keep walking to get to that cabin, and you're going to walk next to me while I distract you from your thoughts." She speaks as though she is certain of her course of action and motions for us to keep going. So, we do.

Brooke decides to tell me a story, so she makes up one as she walks along, her voice soothing my anxiousness and allowing me to focus on each step to get to the cabin. From what I can tell, it sounds like a story about a dog who left his backyard to follow a rabbit and went on an adventure when he realized that there was a secret garden behind his house.

It's ridiculous, and yet I find myself getting lost in her voice and the story. I feel as though she had read through an entire book out loud when she finally finishes, and I can't believe she was able to talk for so long. As she had talked, the pale darkness in the clouds grew slightly darker and the biting of the cold had only grown slightly more painful.

It's much later now, that much I know. I don't know exactly when we left, but we must have been walking for over two hours now since the sun was only about an hour from setting on the horizon when we were looking over the cliff, and now the moon is above us.

"You just talked for somewhere close to two-ish hours. How are you not tired?" I ask her, stunned that her voice hadn't given out. She just shrugs at me.

"It was distracting me too," she says, her teeth chattering as she speaks. She has my flannel buttoned around her torso now with her jacket almost completely zipped up, and I wish more than anything I could just stop and make a fire for her to warm around. Of course, I'm cold too, but I couldn't care less about myself at this moment.

I look ahead, my visibility only getting dimmer and dimmer. I know the general direction of where we need to keep going, but I also know that we need some form of light. I stop Brooke.

"We need to get better visibility. I have the knife, but I'm going to need to get some moss and some sticks. Can you help me look for some?" She hums in agreement, and starts to head off, but I add, "And please don't go too far."

She smiles at me but continues looking at the ground as I remove the knife from my pocket. I lean toward the ground to look for something to help the fire, and the knife in my hand is a reminder of what we could be facing.

And almost as if on cue, I hear a noise I didn't want to hear ever. A growl, and it's close.

"Brooke," I say, my voice low. "Get over here."

She moves quickly to my side. "I heard it too," she says.

It's the dogs again. I know we need to get going, but with our visibility getting dimmer and the danger of the unknown mountains, I'm not sure where we should go. I look around us, hoping to see something—anything—that can help.

Dogs can't climb, so there is one option. If I were to see a cave, I'd be more concerned with what was on the inside than the dogs. If we dig and stay under the snow, we'll certainly die of hypothermia.

But then the growling turns into what sounds like an attack, and it's not on Brooke and me. The sounds get farther away, and I realize we just got really lucky.

Despite all of that, we still have no visibility in this snow, and after spinning around and around looking for something to help us against the dogs, I've lost which direction we came in.

"We need to make those torches now," I say in a low voice. Brooke reveals she had found some dry moss that would work around a large stick, and I see that next to my foot is a large branch. That should do it.

I put together my makeshift torch, wrapping the stock over and over with the moss, then use the knife to break apart some bark and twigs. I sharpen the twigs to a point with the knife and dig a slight hole in the bark, rubbing the twigs together to set a fire. It takes a few minutes, but when it lights, it burns quickly. I know we won't have a lot of time until it burns out, so I light the torches and take Brooke's hand, pointing to a tree with a few notches and a six-foot ledge.

"I need to get higher to see where the cabin is. There's a branch sturdy enough for you to sit on right there until I get back. The dogs can't climb trees, but if they find a way to come after you, throw the fire at them. Fight, Brooke, but I have to get higher, alright?" I know she understands, but she doesn't like that we're separating.

Neither do I. We walk over to the tree, and I hand her the torch. I point to each notch as I climb up to the ledge and she follows in my steps, tossing me the torch in a terrifying feat. I catch it, and when she reaches the ledge, I hand it back to her.

"I'll be back as soon as I can," I say, and she nods but I see the fear in her eyes.

"Be safe, please," she says, shivering as she speaks.

"I will," I say softly, my body trembling as well.

I feel ridiculous, doing the exact same thing my brother did that I had criticized him for, but I don't have a leg injury, I justify. When I start to pull my body upward, I feel understanding flood me by what he meant. He told me he felt like he didn't have a choice, that he needed to protect us. That is more than enough of a reason for me to climb.

As I climb, I think about how when I was younger, Andrew and I used to do this all the time, racing to see who could get to the top the fastest. Then my mom found out that a kid two towns over had fallen off a sycamore and became a quadriplegic. We weren't allowed to climb again.

But I was good. I knew how to climb, knew which steps to skip and which branches would be sturdy enough. And I wasn't afraid of the height.

Now, I fear it, but for a different reason. I can't fail everyone now. I can't leave Brooke alone, my brother and his best friend to die, Emily and Lydia without anyone. I can't do it.

So, I climb hard and fast. I need to get to the top, and soon. The tree isn't nearly as high as some that I have climbed before, and I know that once my head clears the trees above, the moonlight will allow me a glimpse as to where we need to go.

My arms strain as this isn't something I have done since I was a kid, and the cold has made me weaker. I'm also a collegiate snowboarder, and not a seven-year-old who weighed forty pounds. I've put on some muscle and some weight, the muscle helping now but the weight not so much. But I climb harder than I ever did as a kid.

The wood scratches against my fingers and I feel every splinter as it pushes harder into me. Every muscle in my body screams at me for pushing myself harder and higher up the tree. Some notches aren't deep enough, so I have to grab branches to yank myself higher.

The open air above me gets closer, and with each movement of my arms and legs, I feel the tiredness growing. I push and push until I can't push anymore.

Finally, I feel the cool air around me, and I know I have climbed high enough. I look around, noting how high up I am. If I weren't fighting for my life, it would be very pretty up here.

I was right. The moonlight and lack of as many clouds give

me a better picture of where we are in reference to the cabin. What I didn't anticipate, however, was how close we are to it. I must have misjudged the distance or how long we've been walking because the cabin is not far at all. At least one thing is finally going right for us. That's the second time we got lucky tonight.

The sits on top of a smaller hill, and if we were to climb multiple ledges, we would be able to reach it from the base. Walking around the hill, however, would take less time, and it may be an easier climb, depending how slick the snow is.

I carefully descend the tree. My hands continue to splinter as I climb down, but I try to ignore it to the best of my ability. As I near Brooke, I see that by the light of the fire she still holds in her hands, she is relieved.

"Oh, thank goodness. I was so scared you were going to fall out of this tree like Andrew, and I'd be stuck here." She says this in a sort of joking way, but I hear the honesty in it. I was scared too, but not because I feared the fall. I didn't want her stuck here alone either.

"I'm here," I say when I reach her branch. I see that the fire is starting to get closer to the stick, and I know when it does it is going to quickly burn the stick.

"Brooke, I'm going to need you to drop the stick into the snow below us, but not where we're going to climb down. Try to throw it out a bit." She does as I ask. The fire lands in the snow, only burning for a little while longer before dying out.

After it does, I turn to her and say, "I'm going to climb down, and you can follow. I'll help you down." I maneuver around her to find the notches in the tree I used to climb up.

When I descend, she follows behind me, and once I'm at the bottom, I help her down by grabbing her waist. She weighs almost nothing, even for her small frame so it's easy.

I set her down in the snow and stand still for a moment, savoring the few seconds we have of peace before I remove my hands from her and point in the direction we need to head in.

"It's close. Like less than half a mile. I must have misjudged the distance or how long we've been walking. There is a hill that it sits on and a few ledges we could climb to get to it but climbing up the slope itself seems like it might be easier and faster. What do you think?"

"The hill," she says quickly.

"We need to move now then," I say. I don't want to waste any time, and I know she doesn't either. Even if that weren't the biggest problem, the wild dogs are nearby.

Brooke must agree since she starts in the direction I had pointed. We're no longer walking slowly or carefully—we're moving as fast as our legs would take us, despite the snow on the ground holding us down like quicksand.

The hill appears in the near distance, but the falling snow makes it hard to get a good look. Brooke grabs my hand, making sure she doesn't get lost, or maybe to make sure she doesn't lose me. Either way, her hand clutches mine as we move through the deep snow.

It feels like hours pass as we try to get to the slope, but it can't be more than ten minutes. I can't feel my feet at this point, and Brooke is shivering more and more. But what I am really thinking about is that cabin. What happens if there's nothing there that can save us? What happens if we're stuck in the middle of the snowstorm while our friends and my brother are dying on the side of the mountain?

I shake my head to try to get rid of these thoughts, and as I do, Brooke and I pull up to the side of this slope. I can see an area where a car could drive up to the cabin, and part of me wonders: if I look in the opposite direction, will I see a path back to civilization?

We start to walk up the hill that we realize is a long driveway, lifting our legs higher and higher as it is covered in inches of snow. We're both getting tired, really tired, and if we don't make it to this cabin in time, I fear we might collapse.

It takes everything in me to keep lifting my legs. I feel the pain in my calves and at this point I fear I have frostbite on my toes. Despite all of this, I pull myself forward, still clutching Brooke's hand and dragging her forward too. The climb up the driveway is long and hard, and more than ever I feel the weakness in my body.

But then my hand hits something made of wood, and I look forward, seeing a gate in front of me.

We made it.

The gate is iced over, but I can hop it as it is low enough. When I get to the other side, I help Brooke over and we rush to the door. I try to move the handle, but it doesn't budge. Brooke is looking for something—a key, perhaps—but we don't have time, so I kick the door.

Because we aren't in a movie and because the cold iced the locks over, it doesn't budge after the first kick, so I kick it three times more. The door moves slightly, and I figure one more kick ought to be good. I pull back and kick hard, pushing into my heel, and the door swings inside, crashing against the wall.

Brooke and I rush in, closing the door behind us and basking in the warmth of the indoors, something we haven't had the pleasure of for many days now. I'm leaning against the door, heaving hard and trying to catch my breath.

The house is dark, and when my hand hits a switch, I assume is for the lights for the house, the lights flicker, but burn out. It must be because of the storm.

In hopes that anyone with a home in the mountains has a backup generator, I flip the switch on and off again once more, and the lights flicker on. Just when they look like they're about to burn out, a roar comes to life from another room in the house where the generator must be, and the lights stay on.

That is the third time tonight we have been lucky.

Quickly, Brooke and I look around trying to find something—anything—to contact the outside world with. Brooke walks into a room across from the one we're in, and I look around where we entered. I don't see a phone, not that I think we would get any kind of reception up here, but I was hoping for something.

I move around the room, seeing that there is a hallway off the other end of the room that leads to two bedrooms and a garage. From the glances I took, the garage houses the generator we heard come to life minutes before, and the two bedrooms look untouched, both without any kind of communicative device. Seeing nothing that can help us, I walk back into the main room, only to find that Brooke is now looking around.

"Nothing, huh?" I ask, feeling a bit defeated. She shakes her head.

This was my greatest fear. We came all this way, and for nothing. My brother and his best friend are dying on the side of a mountain, and nothing. Panic starts to rise in my chest, but I won't allow it to come through.

There can't be nothing.

This house had a backup generator. There's no way someone with a backup generator doesn't have something else to help them if they got stuck in a storm. I walk back down the hallway, Brooke following behind me. When I enter the garage, I start opening every cabinet that I can find, searching for literally anything.

And then I see it: a satellite radio, one that my grandfather showed me how to use when I was a little boy growing up. Our rescue.

Brooke sees it at the same time as I do, and looking at her, I think she might be about to cry. I think I might too.

I twist the knob at the top and hear it power to life, and I don't think I have ever heard something that made me so grateful. Brooke walks over to me, hugging me around my waist as I press the talk button.

"Hello. My name is Jackson Carter. I am a survivor of a car accident that sent me, my twin brother Andrew, and my friends Brooke, Lucas, and Lydia over the mountainside of US 550 several days ago. We're alive, but my brother and Lucas need immediate medical attention. The members of the other car have passed away, leaving their five-year-old daughter Emily with us." I inhale deeply, sharply, before continuing.

"We went off the mountainside with about an hour and a half, without traffic, left to Montrose, Colorado. Currently,

Brooke and I have found our way to a cabin that looks a few hours walk from where we crashed. Please send help."

I find myself saying these words over and over. As I repeat them, Brooke hugs me tighter, and I feel her crying against me. Tears of my own start to fall from my eyes as I speak, and the panic from earlier still tries to find its way forward.

Then a voice booms through the radio saying, "This is the sheriff's station in Silverton, Colorado. We hear your message and are sending for a search and rescue squad right now. Hold tight." Then static.

Brooke and I cling to each other. *We're saved. We're going to be okay.*

The voice crackles through the radio once more and repeats the message, this time ending with, "If you hear us, let us know you understand."

I press the button, tears streaming down my face, and say, "I hear you. Find us. Please find us."

Time is at a standstill then. The cabin is less warm, but only because my body feels like it sucked all the warmth out. My heartbeat starts to slow, and it's like my movements are stuck in something sticky. I give in, letting my body fall to the hard floor. I hear Brooke shouting, trying to get me to face her and open my eyes.

My eyes are too heavy to open, though, and while I want to assure her that I am alright, I also just want to give into the peace. The silence. No more wind whistling in my ears. No more growling of the wild dogs. No more crying.

Brooke is on my chest now, crying against me. It feels like it takes me forever to open my eyes, but when I do, I see her hugging me against her. My body is sitting up now, and I don't know how I got into this position.

I hate hearing her cry. I hate thinking I made her cry. So, I do the only thing I can think to do: I hug her back. My arms move slowly, but when she realizes I'm moving them at all, she pulls away to look me in the eyes.

"You're okay?" she says breathlessly, hiccupping slightly when she half questions half states her response to my movements. She places a hand on my face, tenderly.

"Yes, nurse," I retort. This earns a small sigh of relief from her, as well as a tiny chuckle, and my heart soars.

She stands up and runs to a cabinet, revealing that she had found some water and a few protein bars. She grabs two bottles and a bar for each of us, and then leans back down to where she was kneeling, handing me one of each.

She then forces me to drink the entire bottle, and when I insist that she needs to drink some too, she says, "Not until you finish the entire bottle." I drink mine quickly then so she will drink hers, and only when we finish the water do we realize how dehydrated we must be. That must be why I fainted, Brooke explains to me. Then we eat the protein bars, slowly since this is the most sustenance we have had in days compared to handfuls of nuts and a sixth of a candy bar.

But then the way she is looking in my eyes fearfully still causes me to hug her hard, harder than I had before. I feel the wetness of my shirt as her tears start to fall again.

"Don't leave me," she says quietly, her words muffled in my

shirt. "I thought you were going to leave me." Her words tug on a string in my heart, unraveling my entire being.

I hold her tighter to me before saying, "I'm right here. I'm not going anywhere, Brooke."

She responds simply. It's only two words, but it is our two words.

"Thank you."

Epilogue

SIX YEARS LATER.

"Next up, number twenty-four, Jackson Carter," the announcer calls from somewhere in the audience. I take a deep breath, urging my board closer to the edge. I feel the cold of the air rushing against my skin, and as I look below me, I remember that day.

I had finally started to compete again for my college, and when I went to the top of the slope, I was starting to panic. I looked into the crowd, and I couldn't see her, but she must have noticed I was freaking out since Brooke stood up and started to wave her arms wildly at me. I saw her, and my nerves immediately calmed down.

Since then, she has been my anchor, and as I continued to compete, even now as a professional, at each competition she was at, she would do the same thing. She is my good luck magnet, and I hate to admit that to myself, but she loves it.

I look out into the crowd now, waiting before I drop in, and see her. Brooke is waving with only one arm, because the other is holding that sweet girl, my daughter, who is waving her own arms above her head.

When Brooke told me we were pregnant a year or so into being married, I was overjoyed. I couldn't wait for a mini version of us to be here. And when she was born, she was everything perfect about her mom, including the blue eyes, brown hair, and beautiful personality. Prior to her birth, I jokingly had said that if she came out looking like her mom, we might as well name her Rosie as that was the nickname I had given Brooke, namely because of her signature scent. Surprisingly, however, Brooke loved the name and we decided that would be her name. Rosie Carter, Ro for short. I wouldn't trade being a father or a husband for anything. I would give up anything for my family.

Next to Brooke and Ro, are Andrew and his wife, along with Emily. Paige was a friend of Brooke's from her internship whom she invited to the wedding, and it was there when Andrew saw her that he knew she was it for him. Two years later, they got married and a few weeks after announced that they were looking to adopt Emily who we had been keeping up with every month since the Christmas following our accident. When they announced their decision, I looked over at Brooke and said, "I told you so." The paperwork went through quickly and the following year Emily was legally part of the Carter family. Now, Emily is eleven and thriving, and we all couldn't be happier.

My eyeline catches Lucas parting through the crowd with a hotdog and letting Lydia step in front of him to hug Brooke and pick up my little girl, spinning her around before placing her at her hip and waving at me. I give her a large grin through my mask, waving back with my mitten.

Lydia was there every moment after the accident for Lucas. She often would drive him to physical therapy and was the first to announce whether he would be joining us for whatever outings we were planning. She stuck by his side, and that proximity was so good for their relationship that the day he realized he could bend down on one knee, he bought a ring and planned a proposal for that weekend. Midway through our junior year, they decided to have a small wedding and have been together ever since. Lydia has been teaching at an elementary school and Lucas decided to get his MBA after graduation. Now, we don't see them as much since they moved to New York for their jobs three years ago. Still, they promised to be here for my final competition of the season, and I was so happy they followed through.

Looking at Ro lean back into Brooke's arms, I remember a few months ago when she asked me why I always looked for her mother when I was about to compete. I explained to her that I was scared.

"Scared?" she repeated after me. "You're never scared." She'd said it so confidently that I almost believed it.

"I am. Every time I am about to drop in, I get scared." I shifted her then so she could see me better.

"There was a time when your mom and I were very scared. She was what brought me out of that. She rescued me from being so scared that I wasn't me."

She gave me a confused face, and I know that at four-and-a-half, she wasn't old enough to completely understand me. But I must have interpreted her look incorrectly because she then elaborated on her response.

"You and Mommy are never scared."

I shook my head. "It's okay to be scared. We were scared. Every time I am about to drop in, I am scared, but your mom helps me to do it. She brings me back, and she reminds me I'm okay."

Something in what I said must have clicked because then she said, "So Mommy helps you to not be scared?"

"Yeah, Ro," I said. "She helps me to not be scared."

I look back at my daughter and wife in the crowd when I see Brooke mouthing the words, "You can do it," and both girls are waving their arms rapidly.

I take a deep breath, inch the board forward, and drop in.

Acknowledgements

There will truly never be enough names, places, influences, etc. on these pages, but I will do my best.

To my teachers, for inspiring me to go beyond the normal senior project. I'm so proud to even be here, and I couldn't have done it without your support.

To my grandma, the one who even inspired me to love reading in the first place. Without you, Grammy, I wouldn't have even known what a joy I would be missing.

To my other grandma, the one who inspired Brooke's compassionate soul. Sitto, you're one of the, if not the, kindest souls to exist. Brooke only holds a match to you.

To my parents, for bearing with me and waiting until the very end to read my book as I requested. I know that couldn't have been easy. Thank you for supporting me in all I do, including writing this book. Thank you for helping me feel comfortable enough to share something that feels so uncomfortable and vulnerable. I love you both.

Dad, when I told you that I didn't like the ending of a book I read as a kid, you told me to write it for myself. You inspired a dream.

Mom, you were my partner in editing this book, unbeknownst to you most of the time. Those late nights in the office working on my book and you doing your work are nights that might seem usual to you, but the time with you was cherished for me. Thank you for that.

To the rest of my family, who I know is always supporting

me in life, and have, for much of my life, consistently supplied me with numerous Barnes and Nobles gift cards to further my addiction. You are all a part of my dreams made reality.

To my grandparents who couldn't be here to hold this book in their hands. I hope you'd both be proud.

To my friends, who were with me every step of the way, even when they didn't know it. There is a piece of all of you in this book. Those who let me rant to them about my excitement, nervousness, etc. about this book—and you know who you are—thank you. Claudia and Mary, specifically, you two are my besties through and through. Thank you for getting so excited with me and cheering me on every step of the way. I love you both so much.

To my dog Jack, who willingly endured my emotional rollercoaster whilst writing and editing this book.

To my lovely editor, Taylor, and my beta reader, Belle. They gave me indispensable knowledge as to how to make my multiple copies that much better. Y'all should be thanking them too.

To Target, for the super comfortable pajamas and sweatpants that I wore much of the time while writing this book. You're a real one.

To Barnes and Nobles, for being the ultimate happy place for me, and for housing all the books that I currently do, and hope to, one day own. Physical copies of books are superior in my opinion. I hope you are around forever.

To LUSH, for inspiring Brooke's hair scent and the name of one of the characters.

Thank you to Muldoon's Irish Pub and Greenleaf

Chopshop, for supplying me with the best salads, outdoor seating, and staff who knew my order by heart. I literally couldn't have written in better environments.

To Spotify for gifting me with the ability to dream of the world my characters are from.

To Ed Sheeran, One Direction, The Fray, The Joy Formidable, Arctic Monkeys, Morgan Wallen, MNDR, Taylor Swift, Russell Dickerson, Kodaline, Sia, Ron Pope, Ross Copperman, Luke Combs, Cage the Elephant, M83, Matchbox Twenty, One Republic, and so many other artists for inspiring the relationship between my characters, and their stories.

To Harry Styles. Honestly, I've just always wanted to thank Harry Styles for something, and now is as good a time as ever. Keep doing what you're doing, Harry.

To Kathleen—You will never know how big of an impact you have made on me. I hope this gives you a little taste.

To Brooke and Jackson. Each of you has a piece of my heart.

To God, for the gift of being creative, to write, and to dream. What gifts those are indeed.

Lastly, thank you to the readers. I've been one of you for so long that it feels wrong to not include you. Thank you for being you. If only one person were to pick up this book and feel something, it would all be worth it. Thanks for picking up my book—I hope it made you happy.

About the Author and *We Aren't Finished Surviving*

Gabriella Ganem was born and raised in Newport Coast, California, and is currently a freshman in college at Biola University in La Mirada, California. She loves to be with her friends, watch all things Marvel, play with her dog Jack, and of course, read and write.

Growing up, Gabriella's grandmother lived on the opposite coast, 2500 miles away from her, so to keep in touch constantly they started a Skype video chat weekly to read a book starting at a very young age. Her grandmother was an English teacher for the majority of her life, and as such found reading to be essential to life. This was passed on to Gabriella and furthered a love for reading and writing all throughout her life.

In junior year of high school, a mere three months before COVID-19 shutdown the USA, Gabriella was approved 501(c)3 status over a nonprofit she started called Kidzstack, aimed at connecting the community to kids who are in need of literature. Inspired by her love for reading and desire for others to share in that, Kidzstack was born, and throughout the pandemic shutdown, Kidzstack thrived, bringing in 2000 books in just a few book drives.

Then, in August of 2020 Gabriella was involved in an accident. Following the actual collision, Gabriella was starting to learn more about what she wanted out of life, her own psychology in relation to trauma, and how to process what it meant to continue life after something that changes everything.

Going into her senior year of high school, Gabriella was encouraged to use these thoughts to spur her senior project: writing a book about trauma and life after it.

We Aren't Finished Surviving was a year-long project intended to be a bit more than just the average senior project, aimed at completing an honors-level and presentation worthy design in the STEM focus. Gabriella chose to center her fiction book on PTSD, trauma, and the effects while in and after the event that caused the psychological changes. Lots of research went into the project, looking into books such as *Turtles All the Way Down* by John Green, *Girl Underwater* by Claire Kells (who's model for the back-and-forth chapters Gabriella added as a component to her own book), and many others.

After months of research, Gabriella started the endeavor of writing her book on April 1, 2021. Following the Camp NaNoWriMo platform's thirty-days of writing to reach 50,000 words, Gabriella was able to complete the entire project with a grand total of 50,500 words in 28 days. The rest of the month of May was used for editing and preparing to present a research articulation on PTSD, and in June the project was complete.

Gabriella decided she wanted to publish *We Aren't Finished Surviving* following the presentation, and spent the summer, fall, and winter editing, hiring a full-time editor (shout out to Taylor) and beta reader (shout out to Belle), and revising, revising, revising. Finally, in March 2022, Gabriella was able to submit her book as completed, and spent her free time designing her own book cover and having fun preparing for her book to be released.

Made in the USA
Las Vegas, NV
14 June 2022

50250516R00141